I0770138

She Whispered through the Woods

BOOK 1 OF THE WAITING TRILOGY

SARA FRANCIS

SF PUBLISHING & MEDIA
sara-francis.com

ISBN: 979-8-9897627-0-5
First edition © May 2023
Cover design by Sara Francis © 2023
Logo artwork © Sara Francis
Book design by Sara Francis

First Edition: January 2024

She Whispered through the Woods

BOOK 1 OF THE WAITING TRILOGY

SARA FRANCIS

SF PUBLISHING & MEDIA
sara-francis.com

This is a work of fiction. Names, characters, places, and incidents either are the product of the author's imagination or are used fictitiously, and any resemblance to actual persons, living or dead, business establishments, events, or locales is entirely coincidental.

ISBN: 979-8-9897627-0-5
First edition © May 2023
Cover design by Sara Francis © 2023
Logo artwork © Sara Francis
Book design by Sara Francis

First Edition: January 2024

To Paul, the man I would wait a lifetime for.

August 2

11:58 PM

"I've been waiting."

August 3

Everything is backward at Camp Southpaw. Breakfast is eaten for dinner, morning prayer is midday, the left-handed outweigh the right, and everyone is referred to by their last names.

Except for me.

"Yo, Second!" my co-counselor shouted this morning, pounding his fist against my cabin door. "Time to get up, man. The kids are coming."

I grumbled and rolled over in my cot. His harsh knocking and the creaking springs should have been strong enough to shove away my exhaustion.

But a whisper kept me up all night: *I've been waiting.*

"It's only anxiety," I repeated to myself from 1 am to 5 am. There was no girl calling out to me in an empty cabin. I told myself the sound was a past memory of my little sister the first time I left for Camp Southpaw. She groaned and whined for me not to leave her for the entire summer. Homesickness struck every counselor as they waited for the sessions to begin. I was a little stir crazy in the interim before the final campers of the year arrived. Perhaps my anxiety spiked because I am returning home next week. I'm convinced it's all in my head. Yes, just in my head.

Peeling away the thin covers, I slid on my flip flops and grabbed my toiletry bag. The frantic knocking became a rhythmic beat. The grumbling voice of my co-counselor rose and fell along a musical staff of flat notes: *"Captain Second, time to go. I want to shower before they come."*

I slung the bag over my shoulder. Tightening my eye patch, I swung open the door.

Anderson stumbled forward into my cabin. His loud beckoning song overpowered my footsteps. Staggering to his feet, he chuckled. "Whatsamattah? You didn't like my serenade?"

"If it rhymed, I might've given it a chance." I taunted.

"Well, not everyone's a writer-guy, or whatever you call yourself." Anderson picked up his bag, leaving an imprint in the blanket of dust on my cabin porch. "Would you give it another chance some time—or should I say," his eyebrows raised, "a 'Second' chance?"

That wasn't the first time I heard that. My nickname caught fire when I first attended Southpaw as a camper in high school five years ago. I'm the second person to hold my name. My father is the first. So rather than being called junior, I've accepted the name of Second.

Exhaustion controlled my emotions that morning. Normally, I'd find a witty reply or mock my co-counselor.

But the only words playing in my head were hers. *I've been waiting.* Her whisper echoed in my brain like a shout between canyon walls.

No, it's only my sister, I thought. There is not another girl.

As each moment passed, I found it harder to believe.

6:02 AM

The dawn painted the green mountains orange. Warm sun rays sliced through the pines like arrows shooting for a target. The Green Mountains of Vermont walled in Camp Southpaw. It was the perfect place to escape. Three months in the wilderness with no contact with the outside world.

Something I desperately needed. I am not looking forward to going back home next week.

Crisp morning air stung my cheeks as we walked from the cabins to the communal bathrooms. Bumps raised over my bare skin, but I welcomed the refreshing chill.

Anderson groaned as he dragged his bag across the dirt. Dark circles deepened beneath his eyes. "Dude, I would *kill* for a coffee right now."

I sucked back a yawn. "I'll be an accomplice as long as a sticky bun comes with it."

"You'd do *anything* for a sticky bun," Anderson retorted as he swatted leaves on low-hanging branches. One caught in his curly brown hair. He didn't notice, and I was too tired to tell him.

He wasn't wrong. I am a sucker for sweets: sticky buns in particular. Their squishy round dough, the frosted glaze that covers your fingers when you ate it, the way it melted in your mouth.

My stomach growled like a bobcat.

"Dude, same." Anderson whined. "But I have to take a *tish*, so food will have to wait."

I snorted. "I'm surprised. You usually break the no-cursing rule by the last session."

A part of Camp Southpaw's mission was to build up its campers in four respects: spiritually, physically, mentally, and socially. Falling into the mental and social category was "proper speech". The counselors had to refrain from swearing and inappropriate language to be a better example to the kids.

But we needed a little color to our vocabulary, so Anderson, a few friends, and I made up the *Southpaw Safe Swears*: words to use instead of the real ones so no one would get punished. At least that was the hope. We haven't been caught yet.

Anderson scoffed. "For *ducks* sake, Second, have little faith in me. We've been co-counselors for how long?"

Before I could reply, the cold stone bathroom building came into sight. Anderson picked up the pace.

I watched the trees sway in the wind. Their leaves went in and out of my vision like scurrying mice.

I took a deep breath, taking in my surroundings. I perceived the world differently. I'm not saying that like a moody guy that needs to be understood.

Seeing the world with only one eye after having two is *weird*.

Perspectives warped and colors faded. It feels like peering through a captain's looking glass all day, every day. Getting used to the headaches was a challenge, but now I'm numb to it.

Am I insecure about the fact that I need an eyepatch to cover a past mistake? Only in the real world. At Camp Southpaw, it's a part of me. All my previous campers thought I was the coolest counselor ever. Captain Second: a hiking legend. The only 24-year-old (that they knew of) who hiked the Vermont 5 in one day. I was proud to wear the eyepatch if it connected me with something good I've done.

They didn't need to know where my lack of sight came from.

No one did.

8:09 AM

The thick aroma of steak cut through the stuffy air of the dining hall. My mouth watered as I grabbed a tray and followed Anderson to the counter. Dinner for breakfast: a normalcy at Camp Southpaw.

"One thing I'll never complain about is the food," Anderson said over his shoulder as he took a plate of sliced medium rare steak, scrambled eggs, potatoes, and bacon from the chef. "Steak for breakfast? I'd forfeit pancakes any day."

"Speak for yourself," I replied, taking my share. "Give me a sugar-high to start the morning."

Anderson stuffed his cheeks with a corn muffin. "You can't hike 10 miles with a doughnut and espresso sitting in your stomach," he mumbled with his mouth full.

"I mean, you *can* but it isn't recommended." I countered.

My co-counselor rolled his eyes and jerked his chin to the tables. I followed him to a long bench where two familiar faces sat enjoying breakfast.

"Aye, Captains!" Sparks waved to me. "Ahoy, Second. How is the Black Pearl doing?"

I dropped my tray on the weathered mahogany table and sat beside Anderson. "If I was a pirate with an actual ship, I wouldn't be sitting here with you three."

Sparks scoffed and ran a hand through his ginger hair. "Puh-lease, I'd be your first mate."

"No way, you'd be swabbing the *poop* deck," Anderson mocked, overly emphasizing his favorite word.

Bancroft scoffed but said nothing. His fingers moved like lightning around his favorite puzzle cube. A man of little words, but his sound effects spoke louder.

"Say all you want, man, but I am clearly the favorite of our Pack," Sparks retorted.

"Mmhmm," Bancroft replied, placing his completed puzzle down red side up. He stabbed a piece of steak with a fork and tore it with his perfect teeth.

The silent retort offended Sparks, but he chose not to argue.

Rolling his eyes, he quieted for a moment to sip his orange juice.

Sparks and Bancroft had been co-captains for years. Lightning and thunder. Sparks: a hyper frat boy with freckles that the girls adored–so he claims. He's never had a girlfriend so clearly he needs to invoke his Irish side to give him more freckles.

Bancroft: a man of few words… probably because Sparks doesn't let him get a word in edgewise. But one sound effect and a look in his dark eyes is enough to say what he needs. His puzzle cube looks as small as an acorn in his strong black hands. He's never seen without it. The co-captains are opposites who became brothers after their first week at Southpaw.

I sure have a weird group of friends. But they're my friends, so I guess that's all the matters.

"I don't think I'd choose any of you to be my first mate," I said. "You can all be cabin boys."

Anderson and Sparks booed while Bancroft shrugged his shoulders.

"Technically, we're all captains, but you're the only one to pass for an actual pirate." Anderson squeezed one eye shut and wielded a plastic knife.

Before I could retort, there was a rhythmic hollow beat. *1 2* and *3 4*

1 2, we responded, banging each hand on the table once.

Turning around on the bench, I faced the camp director who stood at the front of the room.

Director Carter was a strong man with a soft face. His thick brown arms could tear a log in two, but his kind eyes said he wouldn't hurt a fly.

"Good morning, captains!" Director Carter began. "Welcome to your first session at Camp Southpaw." After a brief applause, he continued, "Your final pack of Cubs are en route as we speak. Their daily schedules are in the welcome packets you should have received when you arrived." He swatted the stack of freshly printed papers in his hand. "Keep their emergency contacts close, as you know. I will go over the schedule in full before dismissing you to greet your cubs."

Around that time, I pulled out my notebook to document my day so far. I know I won't need evidence from this morning. I doubt I'll get into another near-fatal accident between breakfast and meeting the cubs...

Director Carter's speech faded as I wrote in my notebook. I barely paid any attention. I'm a veteran captain. I knew the drill. Cubs arrived, we did introductions, ice breakers, Pack-v-Pack game, dinner, campfire, then an overview of the next day before bed. Each day following was set as breakfast, outdoor activity, formation, dinner, campfire, bed, repeat. Same format, but the list of events varied. The routine can get a little boring, but thankfully I have one big event to look forward to.

The mountain climbing expedition.

Yes, for the first time, I'll be leading my Cubs up different trails to do rock scrambling, mountain climbing, and more dangerous outdoor camping experiences.

It is as much pressure as it sounds. Anderson and I will be responsible for the safety of 12 boys in the wilderness. At one point, we'll be in the woods for about six days. No cell service, no buildings, no directors.

Just me, Anderson, the boys, and the woods.

Am I nervous? Only with the fact that we leave August 5th—in two days. Ours is the last long hike of the season. The other packs (groups) have shorter journeys. My job is to get acquainted with and prepare 12 boys—who may not even want to be here—to climb a mountain and live out in the woods for about a week.

So, yeah. No pressure.

As Director Carter discussed the check-in process, Anderson peered over my shoulder to read my journal entry.

"Ay, Second. Why are you so literate," Anderson whispered.

"One of us has to be the smart one." I retorted.

He then proceeded to try and rip the pen out of my hand. I turned away and continued writing.

Am I a little dramatic with my journal entries? Do I describe things too much? I guess. But after you've had an experience like mine, you learn not to leave anything out. The tiniest details tell the biggest stories.

Anderson, shut up. I'm not explaining myself. Stop reading while I write. You'll get us in trouble. No, I won't give it.

As long as you continue to peer over my shoulder, I'm only going to reply to you in my trashy handwriting.

You're the little *tish*-head, not me.

Director Carter is done. Go pick up your stuff, Anderson. We're moving out.

11:57 AM

Waiting is the worst part. The cubs filed in slowly through check-in. Some boys clung to their parents, crying they didn't want to go. Others dropped their stuff in the grass and raced to find their friends from past years. Either way it still takes a while.

I wonder how long *she's* been waiting?

I have to stop thinking about that. The girl whose whisper kept me awake isn't real. She's not waiting for me. She's not waiting for anything.

And yet, she sounded so real. So sincere. I heard her voice clear as a bell at least twelve times last night. It was as if I could speak aloud and reply to her.

I'm so pathetic. Am I that desperate that I'm making things up? Or is my brain so traumatized by the past it's playing this cruel trick?

Whatever. I don't give a *duck*.

Looks like our campers are lined up. Let's see what this bunch of boys bring to my final camp session of the year.

1:03 PM

God has a funny sense of humor. He knows that I am responsible for one of the toughest hiking expeditions. He knows I need kids who have the following qualities as a minimum: mature, well behaved, and willing to participate.

Anderson and my cubs have none of those.

They're immature, off-the-wall, reluctant 15-year-olds who would rather watch paint dry than hold a coherent conversation with Anderson or me.

How are these kids going to trek through the woods and up the side of a mountain?

They arrived approximately around noon. As soon as the first one pulled up, I knew he was trouble. Kicking up dust as he walked, rolling his eyes at every counselor's remark, and the consistent glares were proof enough.

When the boy approached, Anderson ignored the dirty look and cheerfully said, "And your last name, sir?"

"Glover," he grumbled, picking at pollen that stuck to his ripped black t-shirt.

"Aight, Glover, looks like you're with us this session as part of Pack Cottontail." Anderson stuck out a hand. "I'm Captain Anderson."

His hand was promptly ignored, so I waved. "You can call me Captain Second." I greeted with a smile, handing him his welcome packet. "After your folks settle you in, meet back at the handcraft area for a pack introduction."

Glover snatched the papers and peered at my eyepatch. "What are we, five?" He scoffed. "Just because they call you captains doesn't mean you have to dress like one." He shook his head and stormed off to leave his things in the cabin.

I rolled my eye. "Nice kid," I muttered.

"He'll warm up, I'm sure." Anderson scratched his name off the list and wrote some notes beneath his emergency contact info. "Once he realizes there is no wifi, he'll be nice out of need for survival."

"Unless he prefers survival of the fittest," I retorted.

Anderson chuckled. "In that case, we have nothing to worry about."

The next cubs to show up were not as bitter, but honestly, not as enthusiastic. Some, frankly, were not as bright. Not bad boys, just not the best.

Although, my idea of the best are mature boys who won't complain, are skilled hikers, and make their captains look good.

So, maybe my idea of the best isn't the best.

The three-hour arrival window went by like water dripping from a leaky hose. I doodled, edited some of these entries, and chatted with Anderson—who wanted to add crude doodles to my journal. I denied him that satisfaction.

Finally, we scratched off the last name. It is now about 4 pm. Grabbing our belongings, Anderson and I left to meet the cubs at the Handcraft Cabin.

I hoped their moods improved, but I wasn't going to hold my breath.

4:36 PM

The Handcraft Cabin overlooks Lake Solid—as does most of the camp. Camp Southpaw's home base is nestled in the valley. Lake Solid at its front and the forest at its back. It was quiet. Serene.

Well, it was until we arrived where our campers waited.

Since the Handcraft Cabin was so small, all the boys waited outside. They had no notion of how loud they were—or if they did, they didn't care. They shouted and bickered over the most ridiculous things at their highest volume. Their voices bounced off the forest behind us and then skipped across the lake. Director Carter could probably hear us from the other side.

The supervisor overseeing them until our arrival was not pleased. Steam floated from his ears, and his tight face burned red.

He did a double take when we walked over. "Thank the Lord," he mumbled as he ran off without a word.

"Lovely chap, ain't he?" Anderson joked as he watched the counselor book it towards the dining hall.

The kids made no effort to quiet down when we approached. It took me three shouts before they at least looked in our direction. When they noticed the eyepatch, their loud bickering became murmurs and chuckles.

"Welcome to Camp Southpaw," I began, ignoring their comments. "I am Captain Second. With me is Captain Anderson. We're your counselors for the next two weeks in Cabin Cottontail."

The murmurs continued, but no outward response.

"You're probably hungry, so let's get this over with, okay?" Anderson pulled out his packet and began calling the names:

Atkins, Cline, Fischer, Glover, Hart, Huerta, Madden, Moss, Ortiz, Pierce, Sweeney, Weaver.

One by one, they responded. Somewhat. If it wasn't an obnoxious *"I'm here!"* it was a grunt.

Just from their answers and behaviors during the ice breakers, I could point out the troublemakers.

I'm sure I can charm a few to get on our side quickly. I think of myself as a pretty likable guy with the campers. I also don't have to worry about all twelve at once. Anderson and I split the boys up, so I'll only deal with Atkins, Cline, Glover, Huerta, Pierce, and Sweeney.

The painful introductions ended, and I explained our upcoming expedition. Attitudes shifted for better and for worse.

"If you've been to Camp Southpaw, you know each session gets one big trip that ventures outside the camp," I began. "The day after tomorrow, we will be making our six-day trek up Mount Donwanago."

Thankfully, there were more "*whoops*" than complaints. At first, I thought I misjudged the boys. I thought perhaps it would be a decent group after all.

Then, a boy, Huerta, with greasy hair and tan skin started asking dumb questions. "How do we know you're not going to just ditch us for *tishes* and giggles?" He jerked his chin toward me. "You seem like the captain to abandon his crew." Every word dripped with sarcasm.

Although proud the cub knew Camp Slang, his attitude ticked me off. I had been taunted multiple times for my eyepatch—which is a natural response that I had no patience for.

I crossed my arms. "Because I don't have time for a lawsuit, Huerta. Just like I don't have time for stupid questions."

I got one chuckle from a scrawny boy with a sharp nose: Pierce. He stood beside Huerta who elbowed him for laughing at my reply.

"We will go over more details tomorrow, but the gist is this." I put my hands together, gesturing after each word as I explained, "Hike, climb, eat, sleep, repeat. Easy?"

Huerta wanted to speak again, but Anderson shot him a look. The cub rolled his eyes, and no one said another word.

"Good," Anderson exclaimed, clapping his hands. "Now, let's go eat."

Anderson waved the boys to file in a not-straight line behind him. In a not-orderly fashion, they made their way away from the Handcraft Cabin and toward the dining hall.

I tailed behind, ensuring no campers were stupid enough to run amok.

As we left the Handcraft Cabin, a gust of wind whisked out of the woods. It was warm like the summer but a chill shot through my bones. A whiff of lavender and pine filled my nostrils. It was unique.

Unnerving. Hair stood up on the back of my neck. I felt someone watching me from the forest.

Waiting for me.

I whipped around. Branches tremored as the wind stopped suddenly. Unnaturally. Peering closer, I sought out a bird that perhaps dove into the trees. Nothing but the green grass, brown bark, and wide leaves.

Convincing myself it was nothing, I turned away to follow my Cubs.

Then, I felt it again. The breeze pressed at my back like a soft hand. A comforting touch that made me want to turn around and accept an embrace.

Only every time I looked over my shoulder, the feeling vanished, and the forest went still. I picked up the pace and followed my Cubs back to the dining hall.

Something followed me in the woods. It wanted me but I wasn't so sure if I wanted it.

Now that I write this out, I guess I'm not so sure *yet*.

7:38 PM

Dinner: one thing captains and their cubs could bond over.

A feast awaited us in the dining hall. Waffles served with fried chicken, protein pancakes, bacon, sausage, and everything else a breakfast buffet would feature.

Like I said, everything is backward at Camp Southpaw.

None of the boys complained about the food. Their sticky fingers and messy mouths were a testament to the chef's abilities. The only complaint I had was that there were no sticky buns. They were a rarity at Camp Southpaw, but the pride and joy of the kitchen. I begged for them at the start of every session. But alas, the staff's priority of creating delicious meals for the entire camp—not to mention taking dietary needs into consideration—prevented them from making my sweet delights.

Sorry, I get super dramatic when I'm hungry.

I couldn't satisfy my growling stomach until Sweeney received his special dish. I stood beside him at the counter as the kitchen staff whipped a gluten-friendly batch of eggs and bacon.

The bull of a boy looked like he could squish Pierce if he sat on him. But looks had been deceiving. His cheeks reddened as he awkwardly awaited his meal. His pudgy fingers fiddled with the strap around his white instant-print camera.

As I peered over the counter to see his dinner's progress, the bright flash went off. White sparked my vision. I clenched my jaw and sucked in a quick breath. Memories I hated flooded to the front of my mind:

Lights.

Glass.

Sirens.

Screams.

Blood.

I shook my head hard and pressed a hand over my eyepatch. My racing heart pounded in my chest. Not now. Not now, I repeated to myself I took in a few deep breaths and pushed the memories away. I had been safe for months. My mind was clear for months. Camp was my safe haven; I would *not* let anything resurface here.

Sweeney said nothing, kept his eyes down, and quietly re-clipped his camera onto his bag.

After the chefs handed off the steaming dish, I brought Sweeney back to the table to chat with the cubs as if nothing happened.

They asked a hundred and ten questions. When were we going on the trip? What would we eat for food? Did we really have to hike that long? What if it rained?

"When has rain ever stopped us at Southpaw?" I asked, tearing into a piece of chicken. The meat warmed my mouth. Savory with a touch of sweet from the fresh Vermont maple syrup I lathered on it.

What can I say? I'm a *sweet* guy. In every way.

"Rain soaked through my boots once and I almost got hypothermia." Cline complained. His tight voice and thick glasses stereotyped him as a nerd. "Do you know how to cure hypothermia?"

Anderson chuckled. "That's why you bring two pairs of shoes and a ton of socks."

"He's also a klutz and fell in puddles." Atkins garbled with a mouth full of pancakes. He swallowed and elbowed Cline so hard I thought a rib would snap. "We were in the same pack last year, so I know what I'm talking about."

Cline's face reddened, and he slurped his apple juice.

I shook my head. "Regardless, we'll make sure you're more prepared." I waved my fork down the table. "We have a small hike tomorrow and then we pack for the big day."

Most of the kids looked forward to the trip. My "favorite" camper (sarcasm overload) did not.

Glover tore at his waffle and grumbled, "How can we trust a guy who can barely see?"

My juice went down the wrong pipe. After a few harsh coughs and unhelpful pats from Anderson, I looked at the boy and stated, "Experience, that's how."

Glover rolled his eyes and muttered something only the boys beside him could hear. They looked at me and then back at Glover. A silent understanding between them. What were they hiding? An inside joke? A secret?

Ugh, secrets. Something I've always hated. Secrets tore my life apart. The secret and mystery behind my eyepatch were the reasons Glover doubted me now. I was sure of it.

I shook my head hard. I couldn't get so worked up over a cub. I am a captain. I was chosen specifically to take these twelve kids on a six-day expedition. That counted for something.

I glanced down at my watch. Almost 7:45. Time to clean up.

After we cleared our tables, we brought them back to the cabins to grab jackets. We had extra time to kill, so I wrote these latest two entries sitting on Pack Cottontail's cabin porch. The time stamps are approximate. Then again, everything is approximate. I document everything a little bit after it happens.

The pain-in-the-*brass*, Glover, saw me writing and tried to make a comment but Huerta called him over.

Ugh, I don't know why that kid gets under my skin. I mean, the comments are rude and the jabs toward my condition are frustrating. I just cannot forget where I am. It's my job to better these kids. To help them grow up.

Although it's hard when I don't feel so grown up myself sometimes. I don't even know what I want to do when I get back home after the summer is over. I had a chance at a nice career, but *she* botched that. I am quite a talented fellow since I have a knack to find people who ruin every opportunity.

Even with annoying cubs, the summer camp is my safe haven. I'd stay here forever if I could. Not having to worry about being twenty-four and unsure. Not having to worry about finding a job and someone to spend my life with.

Pretty lonely, probably. Safer, definitely.

I wouldn't be able to hurt anyone else ever again.

9:25 PM

It's only anxiety. It's only anxiety. It's only anxiety.

There is no girl calling me from the woods. No whispers. No cries.

Just anxiety. Let me talk myself through this. Where did my anxiety start?

We sat around the campfire on split logs. The boys shifted often to avoid splinters in their butts. We faced our rival group: Pack Coyote led by Sparks and Bancroft. Sparks waved his hands around, telling some dramatic retelling of an event that probably didn't happen. The other cubs sat around Bancroft as he solved his puzzle cube. Faster and faster each time.

Pack Coyote is definitely a worthy opponent. Our battles will be legendary.

Not that we do any real battling. Some water polo, capture the flag, and my favorite: ditch dodgeball.

During certain events, we'll face off with all the other packs— all appropriately named after animals. From left to right around the campfire were Marten, Bobcat, Coyote, Hare, Otter, and Weasel.

None of that would have caused anxiety or made me hear voices. Ugh, what else happened tonight?

Sparks noticed our pack filed in and stopped his story. "Why, Pack Cottontail, do you have the guts to endure my tale?"

"Is it really that bad?" Anderson snorted.

Sparks's brow furrowed. "Very funny. It's actually pretty terrifying."

"Oh, is it a ghost story?" Atkins gasped. He jumped from his seat and ran over to their side. "I love ghost stories." He squeezed his thick frame between two slender campers.

Cline scoffed and crossed his arms. "You wouldn't think a jock would be so obsessed with the paranormal."

"Wait, if you're a football player, how can you not have a girlfriend?" Huerta asked.

"Shut up, guys," Atkins shouted. "There is something about the supernatural that turns me into a nerd."

"As a self-proclaimed nerd, I take offense," Cline called back.

Sparks stood up and looked around at the other packs. Most of the other cubs turned their attention to him. "Wait, does this mean you all want to hear my story?"

Anderson spread his arms out. "You have an audience, so get it over with before Director Carter comes and shuts you up."

Sparks gulped and tugged on the collar of his rust-orange shirt. "O-okay, well you all better be quiet and pay attention. This is a true story that takes place in these very woods."

"Booooooring," one of the boys from Pack Weasel yelled. His supervisor elbowed him, and all attention returned to Pack Coyote's captain.

Sparks closed his eyes and took a deep breath. A long shadow trailed behind him as the sun set. His eyes popped open, and a chilling tale fell from his lips:

"Three wrong words break a heart. Five wrong words consume a soul. Ten wrong words last eternity."

Sparks pointed to Bancroft then to Anderson. "Her age matched the Southpaw Captains'. Young and ready to conquer the world." He lowered his voice. "Until he came along."

"Who?" a boy asked.

Sparks continued in a voice laced with anger, "A man who lied. A man who claimed to love her. But he looked into her emerald eyes and wanted to steal their treasure. He hated her hair of fire. He wanted to douse it until the last ember turned black."

He pressed a hand to his chest. "She was afraid of him, but never told a soul. No matter the bruises. No matter the mental cages. She thought she could change him. Fix him. Save him." He balled his fists and whispered, "But it was too late."

He thrust his hand into the sky. The setting sun colored his skin orange. "On a clear night like this, he brought her to a forest. The leaves swayed in the wind. The air tasted of pine. Her lavender perfume floated along the breeze. The night was beautiful. Romantic." His eyes narrowed. "But there was no love in the forest."

Wiggling his left ring finger, he continued, "The diamond in his hand sparkled, but his grip around her wrist burned." He trailed his fingers down his cheek. "The bruises on her cheek stung. *No more,* she thought. *I will do it no more.*"

"'I hate you.'" Sparks held up three fingers. "Her three words shattered her heart. With hatred in his eyes and evil lacing his tongue, he bellowed, 'Then, you will die here'." Five fingers. "His five words tore her soul."

Sparks paced between the rows of intently listening cubs. "She ran. Wolves howled. Branches snapped beneath her footsteps. His screams grew louder and louder." The captain grabbed Anderson's curls and snarled, "Her fiery hair burned as he yanked her backward. She screamed. No one but the moon heard her pleas."

Anderson kept quiet as Sparks bent forward and whispered, "A sinister face leaned over. A devil's snarl stuck upon his lips." He let go of Anderson and picked up a rock on his left. "He crashed down the first stone." He took another in his right hand. "Then the second." He tossed them down toward the fire. "Rocks rained down until the final breath caught in her throat."

He walked in silence back to his side of the campfire, whispering, "'You'll suffer alone for your afterlife. Forgotten and unloved forever.' Ten words. A curse. A bond." He gripped his wrist. "Her last breath floated from her sweet lips. Beautiful emerald eyes faded. A treasure lost." Pointing to the sky, he continued, "The glowing moon had heard her cries. It could not save her life, but it saved her soul." Sparks wrapped his arms around Bancroft, who ignored him. "It latched onto her heart and hugged it tightly."

Sparks startled the boys as he jumped up and shouted, "Now, she haunts the forest under the moonlight. She waits and waits and waits. One man struck her down in the forest. Now, she waits for another man to pick her up." He pointed a finger at me. "For a worthy gentleman to heal her heart and break her murderer's curse." Sparks came over and put his hands on my shoulders. "She needs someone to love her before she can go home."

The crackling fire screamed after his story. Embers shot up as the wood settled into its hellish flames. Every boy remained silent as Sparks returned to his place.

Atkins clapped slowly. "Dude, that was the coolest ghost story I think I ever heard!" The other boys joined in the applause.

Sparks ran his fingers through his ginger hair. "Thanks, guys. I'm glad you liked it."

"It was scary as *bells* that's for sure," Anderson admitted. "I felt you get into character when you pulled my hair."

Huerta jumped up and clapped frantically. "I officially want to be a ghost hunter now. I say we find that girl and send her home."

"Well, maybe we'll see her during our trip." I teased. I don't know if I'm a big believer in the supernatural. The realistic part of me doesn't think there is a lonely girl in the woods and it's all in my head.

But a voice in my mind never sounded so clear.

"Everyone, settle down!" Director Carter shouted over the clamor as he approached the fire. With a small drum in one hand, he beat *1 2* and *3 4*.

1 2 we responded with claps.

Taking a megaphone from his assistant, he brought it to his lips and shouted, "Thank you, Captain Sparks, for kicking off the session with a new story. Please, no ghost hunting without your captains."

The boys laughed.

"Now," Director Carter continued. "Who is ready for adventure?!"

All the boys whooped and clapped.

"Welcome to Camp Southpaw," he began. "I hope you are ready for a fun, formation-filled session."

As Director Carter went through the general rules of the camp, a few boys tossed logs onto the fire. It crackled and popped. Bits of embers warmed my knees, and the flames twisted up to the stars. Was that it? Did I get anxious about fire? No, that's stupid. That's never happened before. Fire isn't one of my triggers.

The scent of smoke filled my nostrils. I breathed in deep, watching embers float in the wind. They rode their way towards the forest. Fluttering until the sparks slowly faded between the trunks. Except two of them wouldn't dissipate.

The glows hovered and floated in the darkness. They danced along the same plane, spiraling as they left a faint tail of light. The orange embers resembled the sparkling lights of stars. My heart raced as I watched them multiply, fluttering like fireflies. The glow illuminated the branches as they spun further into the forest.

Then, I felt it.

Something in that forest nagged at my heart. It plucked the strings of my soul like a guitar, playing a song I wanted to sing along to. It called me. Cried for me. The embers wanted me to follow them.

I looked around to see if the other boys noticed, but their eyes fixated on Director Carter or each other.

I tried not to look at the embers taunting me. I watched the crackle of the fire in the center, but it was no use. Yellow, red, and white flames entangled, and embers broke free, following their brothers into the woods. My eye observed their journey to join the others. No flames ignited the dry leaves. A peaceful glow illuminated the dark woods.

Director Carter's speech ended, and the camp began its routine nightly campfire songs. The words fell from my lips out of habit, but my focus remained on the flames. They congregated in the trees, wandering back and forth like lost children unsure of which direction to search in. The final song ended, and the embers stopped pacing and hovered above a tree branch.

As the boisterous acclaims of the finale bounced off the campgrounds, I heard it. It was clear as day, sweet as sticky buns, and eerie as the darkness. It shot through the woods, striking me hard and strong.

"I've been waiting."

My breath caught in my throat. It was her. The same girl I heard in my dreams. I coughed as I choked on air, covering my mouth with my elbow. Anderson smacked my back repeatedly. The discomfort meant I wasn't dreaming. Pinching my eye shut, I shook my head hard. On a mental count of three, I looked back into the forest.

Blackness.

The embers disappeared. The voice quieted. The cub's chatter loudened as they rose from their wooden perches. The fire hissed as a captain doused it. Smoke floated across the campground, but no embers accompanied it.

"Yo, Second, let's get moving!" Anderson called.

He made no mention of my apparent distraction. I tailed our cubs back into our cabin to prepare for the night. While Anderson was on bathroom duty, I sat and documented.

This is all too strange not to write down. I'm going to be as descriptive and thorough as possible. That way, when I lose my mind, the therapist can see I was sane at one point.

Well, let's hope I don't go insane. That's not definite, but I feel like I'm on the cusp.

Perhaps this is a result of Sparks' ghost story. Maybe my mind is playing tricks on me, making me think supernatural things exist. Making me think a soul is haunting the forest of Camp Southpaw.

There is only one thing for certain:

The forest is calling to *me*, and I have no idea why.

August 4

"Rise and shine, Cottontails!" Anderson shouted as he goose-stepped down the bunk aisles with me blowing into a harmonica behind him. He sang a jumble of words that didn't rhyme nor resemble a song in any fashion. I have no idea how to play the harmonica, but I'm great at making annoying noises.

A few boys shot up, banging their heads against the bunks above them. Some threw colorful insults. Others rolled over and covered their heads with their pillows.

Honestly, I don't blame them. I wouldn't want to be woken up by the Cottontail Captain Cacophony.

I didn't sleep last night, so the chaotic routine energized me this morning. Every time I closed my eye, I saw the sparks and heard the woods' voice. Then, my imagination ran with the thought that the voice was the ghost from Sparks's story. The girl who was murdered by her psycho fiancé. It creeped me out and kept me awake.

"Why you gotta be like that?" Huerta growled, pulling a sheet over his head. A string of curses hid between his complaints.

"The words you are looking for are '*mama duck*' and 'my *brass*'," I corrected, yanking the sheets off his face.

After shoving the twelve boys out the door, we walked them to the bath house.

The scent of the lake greeted my lungs. I inhaled deeply, keeping my eye fixated on the boys trudging along. Thankfully, the cabins were closer to the water than the woods bordering the camp. However, it took a lot of willpower not to glance over at the forest.

Reaching the bath house, we brought the boys inside to do their thing. I freshened up earlier in the morning when no one was there. I am not a fan of removing my eyepatch in front of others—cubs, especially. Rather than following them inside, I sat in the grass and began to journal.

Right now, I face the lake. The ducks swim gracefully across, quacking their morning tune. They sound better than Anderson and I. But even between their song, the chirping birds, and chilly breeze, I can hear her voice tugging at the back of my head.

"I've been waiting."

I'm refusing to look back.

7:46 AM

"I bet if I drink five cups of coffee, I'll smell colors." Huerta taunted. He dragged his arm across the splintered table, pulling in three mugs that didn't belong to him.

The other boys in my care tossed in slices of bacon and potatoes as their ante for the bet.

"There is only one color you can *actually* smell." I told him, thinking of orange and its distinct sweet citrus aroma. "If you can describe it well enough," I added two strips of steak to the pot, "I'll let you win this round."

Should I have discouraged him? Absolutely. Am I irresponsible at times? Of course. I am a sucker for bets.

Huerta smirked, flashing his dimples. "*No problemo, Capitán.*" His wink was less reassuring than he had probably hoped. To the beat of the boys clapping, the cub gulped down the first cup of coffee. Then the second. Then the third. Beads of brown dribbled down his tan chin.

I didn't have the heart to tell him it was decaffeinated. The only thing he'd smell later is the color yellow from frequent restroom trips.

Huh, I guess that's two colors I associate with smells. Maybe Huerta is onto something.

Breakfast ended and Huerta rushed to the boys' room while we cleaned up.

"Are you cubs ready for your first Southpaw match?" I asked, tossing a napkin into a trashcan.

Pierce shrugged. "I'm ready for whatever."

"I, on the other hand, may need more explanation." Cline butted in. A smudge of gravy smeared his glasses as he tossed a plate. "Is there a lot of physical activity in this match?" He asked, frantically rubbing the lens with his shirt.

Glover scoffed. "You do know you're at a *wilderness* camp, right?" He walked past a mess on the table. "If you can't handle it, just get out of here."

"Glover, we all have different abilities," I scolded, picking up the trash he ignored. "That won't stop anyone from participating."

"Clearly." Jutting his chin out toward me, he covered his eye with his palm. "But sometimes, we need to learn to give up."

I bit my tongue. I couldn't lash out on one of my cubs, no matter how rude they are.

My eyepatch is something unusual for a teenager to see. A young man with one eye is daunting to anyone, frankly. I don't need everyone to be sensitive to it, but I do deserve respect.

Thankfully, Pack Coyote interrupted that "delightful" conversation.

"Are you ready to be eaten by the Coyotes?" Sparks taunted. He laced his fingers behind his head. He looked cool and confident for a captain whose cubs were staring at the ceiling, uninterested and unenthused.

Anderson and the rest of the cubs rejoined us. "Cottontails will outrun Coyotes any day," my co-captain replied, tugging on his stained white t-shirt.

"Actually, a rabbit can only reach twenty five miles an hour while coyotes run thirty five," Cline interjected, pushing his glasses up the bridge of his nose.

"Way to be a buzzkill, buddy." I patted the boy's back.

Atkins wiped syrup on his pants and said, "Captain Sparks, I have to say I'm a huge fan of your story from last night."

Sparks beamed. "I'm glad to see how popular I've become."

"The real question, is that story yours?" Anderson teased.

"It *is* a Sparks's story but just not his," Bancroft scoffed, finishing his puzzle cube for the billionth time that day.

Blood rushed to Sparks's cheeks. "You don't talk much, Bancroft, but when you do, try not to burst my bubble, okay?"

The Coyote Captain smirked and slid his cube red-side up into a leather pouch on his hip. He jerked his head toward the door and made a crescendoing hum.

Already used to his sound effects, the cubs marched outside behind him. Sparks followed after giving us the evil eye.

Huerta returned from the restroom, tugging on his fly. "What did I miss?"

"Just Captain v Captain trash talk," I said. Rubbing my palms together, I smiled. "So, who's ready for Capture the Flag?"

Whoops and chaotic war cries erupted from Pack Cottontail. 99% of the boys ran off with Anderson. Huerta needed to use the bathroom...again. I offered to wait for him while the others got a head start.

He's taking a little while, so I'm finishing my journal entry. Wonder if he's learning what the color brown smells like...

8:15 AM

As I've said, everything is backward at Camp Southpaw. Meaning, our Capture the Flag isn't any normal capture the flag. While the general principle remains the same, the conditions are a little different.

Think a hide-and-seek/dodgeball/capture the flag hybrid. This is the first full camp event of the session. It is meant to help the captains bond with their cubs while sporting some friendly competition.

Like all capture the flags, it involves a flag in need of capturing. With seven groups, each one is designated a rival pack to capture. However, there is one group that become the saboteurs. They can mess with any team they want and are designated by the red bandanas they wear on their arms.

That's not the only twist. Hidden across the campgrounds are buckets of water balloons. Six buckets per pack. You can find them inside *and* outside the gameplay area. The cubs search the main grounds, while the captains venture into the woods. The only way to get another camper out of the game is to hit them with a water balloon.

But once they're hit, they're out. No revivals.

"Would anyone really know if I hit them with a different colored water balloon?" Huerta asked, tying a green bandana around his forehead.

Anderson pulled our flag taut. "Someone would call you out on it. Now, steady Captain Second."

I interlocked my fingers and pressed my back against the building. Anderson pressed one foot into my palms and stepped up, clambering atop the small hut.

One of Anderson's cubs—Madden—cocked his head, watching with wide gray eyes. "Why are we hanging our flag on the girls' bathroom?"

"None of the other cubs know we even have a ladies' room," I explained, handing Anderson nails. "It's within game guidelines, though."

My co-captain shielded his eyes and scanned the campus like a pirate seeking land. "With the forest at our backs and the tents to our right, we will have the sneakiest ambush."

A breeze tickled my neck. I refused to turn around and look into the forest. I knew I would have to face whatever it was when the game began, but I put it off as long as possible.

Extending my arms, I brought the cubs in for a huddle. "All right, I hope you're as competitive as I am."

They eagerly shuffled forward.

Glover's enthusiasm surprised me. His eyes lit up and a mischievous grin spread across his face. "At least competition is one thing we agree on, Captain Second."

"Hopefully soon we'll agree on a bit more," I replied.

Glover squinted. "Don't get ahead of yourself, cyclops."

Huerta chuckled. "Heyyyy, that's a good one!" He clapped my back. "So, what's the plan, Captain Cyclops?"

My ears burned, but I ignored their new name. I explained my brilliant plan.

The camp trumpet blew, signaling the start of the game. The boys scattered to their positions while the captains raced to the starting area.

10:00 AM

Twenty four captains stood in a circle around the flagpole at the center of camp. The green cloth swayed proudly in the wind, showing off Southpaw's logo: a bear footprint.

I spotted Bancroft and Sparks opposite of Anderson and me. A pink bandana wrapped around Bancroft's tree-trunk bicep. Sparks tied it around his forehead, causing his ginger hair to stick up like he had been electrocuted.

Director Carter stood beneath the flagpole, megaphone to his lips and the trumpet at his side. "Captains, are you ready?" His voice echoed across the campgrounds.

We all responded with *whoops* and cheers.

"You know the rules. The other staff and myself will be referees. Play hard, but practice good sportsmanship, ya hear?" He lifted the trumpet close to his mouth for a quick switch. "Ready, set…" Then he blew one long trumpet blast.

I spun on my heel and darted in the opposite direction of our flag.

Camp Southpaw is about 500 acres of gorgeous greenery which means a lot of space to cover. It is a half circle with Lake Solid at its front and the forest at its back. Our flag was northwest of the flagpole. So, naturally I'd go southeast past the Dining Hall and the Health Center.

My game plan was three fold. One: find water balloons in the forest. Two: distract the opposing teams. Three: locate the Coyote's flag.

Kinda simple if you think about it. My explanation sounded way cooler.

I ducked behind the maintenance shed, waiting for some shirtless Cubs to race by screaming like wolves. I looked down at my watch. A little after 10 am. The game maxed out after two hours. Once the cubs passed, I forced my feet to move forward. My brain didn't like that I was going towards the forest. Her voice was haunting.

Look, I don't get scared easily…

I think.

Ugh, who am I kidding. This whole voice thing is freaking me out.

Was it actually a ghost? Was Sparks's story real? Was this voice really a murdered girl who needed a lover to save her?

No. That's stupid. Second… You have anxiety, dude. Just get over it like you always do.

Anyway, so I had to do a lot of convincing to force myself to keep moving.

Balling my fists, I raced to the edge of the woods. Before I could stop and compose myself, I heard the howling of the shirtless campers behind me. Only captains were allowed in the forest, so I had no choice.

I dove into the woods.

The voices faded behind me as I raced uphill. Branches snapped beneath my feet, echoing off the trunks. A dead giveaway to whatever captains lurked about. When I was far enough, I slowed. Hands on my knees, I caught my breath and took in my surroundings.

Painted on a wooden sign was "Mount Donwanago". The starting point of tomorrow's expedition. I always wondered if that's what it was actually called or if it was named by a defiant cub. I had imagined Chief Carter as a boy being brought up the mountain shouting "I don't wanna go!" to his father—the former owner of Camp Southpaw.

The crunching of leaves interrupted my musings. Looking over my shoulder, I checked to see if I was being followed.

A shadow darted behind a trunk.

I sucked in a breath and raced off the trail, heading deeper into the woods. A warm breeze tickled my neck. Chills shot down my spine. A presence followed me closely. If it really was another captain, they took this game to the next level.

I ran uphill for about four minutes before stopping. Sweat dripped down my nose and my blue shirt clung to my lean frame. I felt disheveled and disoriented. Running my fingers through my thick brown hair, I took in my surroundings.

Colored trail markers decorated the trees like badges on a boy scout sash. A tattered wooden sign dangled from a rusty nail; the words barely legible.

The wind blew, swaying the branches above me. A glimmer of light flickered in the distance. A bucket of water balloons. I thought.

The goal in my sights, I raced forward.

But the harder I ran, the further away it seemed to get. The wood grew thicker. Darker. Footsteps echoed behind me, so I didn't look back.

Thin slivers of light cut through the thick leaves. Birdsongs grew louder in my ears. Shouts of the camp grew quiet in the distance as I continued to make my way up.

I pumped my fist when I saw the silver bucket. Green water balloons poured out the top. A few tried to scurry away and escape into the forest.

I snatched up my prize and collected the ones that fell. My cubs needed all the ammunition they could get.

After collecting the last one, I turned to leave the clearing when a warm breeze brushed my lower back. Tingles spread down to my toes. It startled me. Whipping around, I almost called out but held my tongue.

I told myself it was just the wind.

A flock of birds shot into the sky. Air caught in my throat as a silence fell over the forest. It was unnatural. Uncomfortable. My stomach knotted. I caught glimmers of golden light out of the corner of my eye.

Embers danced along a wooden path. Twisting this way and that. Carefree. Their warmth and beauty calmed my trembling hands but didn't stop my beating heart. Dozens of lights ignited in the dark shadows of the woods like fireflies during a summer evening.

Yes, that's what they are, I thought as I watched them line up. They're only fireflies.

My subconscious was not convinced.

Lights danced around my feet, urging me forward. My brain said no, but every nerve said yes.

The silver bucket rattled as I followed the sparkling embers down a hidden footpath. Pine and lavender floated along the breeze. I drank it in. The scents filled my lungs. They were a soft hug after a stressful day. Something I yearned for but never received. The thought of slender arms pulling me close, calming my anxious spirit.

The forest lights paused amidst a clearing before they rose. Gold cut through the evergreens as the different sparkling lines entangled. Each shimmer found a partner. They danced in circles higher and higher until they tickled the treetops.

A voice floated along the breeze. Each consonant precise. Each word purposefully pronounced as if it screamed in my face:

"I've been waiting."

My breath knotted in my chest. My face burned as the voice sang in my ears. It was not sinister. It was not frightening. It was sad. Lonely. Heartbreaking.

My gaze followed the embers. They danced in a circle above me. I twisted around and around, following their movements. My brain rattled in my skull. Pinching my eyes shut, I shook my head hard.

When I looked up, I saw her.

A white glowing figure sat upon a thick trunk. A thin dress swayed around her frame. Thick hair defied gravity around her heart shaped face. The same three words tumbled from her pale lips.

"I've been waiting. I've been waiting. I've been waiting."

Neurons in my brain fired in every direction: run away, run to her, hide away, hug her. White light radiated off her being and I wanted to soak it up with every inch of me. Her soul was stronger than gravity, pulling me toward her. Yanking me forward until I had no control over myself.

I tried to fight back, but it was no use. In seconds, I stood beneath her tree, gazing upon her. She was captivating. Beautiful. Unnatural. Real.

Her translucent skin glistened in the sun. White eyes stared intently, but she never glanced down.

Who was she? Was she the ghost from Sparks's story? Was she a lost soul in need of being sent back to the afterlife?

My lips parted, but no noise came out. I wanted to say something. To let her know I was there, looking up at her. She appeared not to notice me. My heart wanted to speak, but my brain debated between fight or flight.

Clinging to my bucket of water balloons, I slowly stepped away, but couldn't keep my eyes off of her. It was just her and me in the middle of the woods. No cubs, no captains. No birds chirping, no squirrels scampering. The silence sang her sorrowful song.

I never wanted to leave.

But everything I want is taken away from me as fast as it comes.

A trumpet sounded in the distance. I whipped my head around to look in its direction.

When I looked back, she was gone. Whatever peace I felt, she took with her. I had nothing left but the stupid water balloons. With an uneasy mind and a heavy heart, I turned around and raced out of the forest.

I had forgotten about the game. I had forgotten about the camp, my cubs, the other captains, all of it. At that moment, none of that mattered.

But she did.

11:47 AM

"Yo, Captain Second!" Anderson called as I jogged back to my pack. His brown curls stuck to his sweaty forehead. Water balloon pieces clung to his tan shoulders like seaweed on sand. He reeked of sweat and latex. "Where the *duck* were you, man? We could've used the backup!"

I barely heard him as I stood in the center of the field. The sweet voice of the Ghost Girl rang in my head. Her hair floated in front of my eye. She was all I saw.

"Uhh, Earth to Second?" A hand waved in front of my face.

I shook my head hard. Realizing I still cradled the water balloons, I pushed them away from me. "Here you go," I mumbled.

Anderson arched an eyebrow. "Are you okay? You were gone for the entire game."

"The game started at ten, and I ran to get our team's balloons in the forest," I recounted. "I was only gone for a half an hour."

My co-captain looked at his watch. "Dude, it's 11:47."

I clicked my tongue. "Pretty sure your watch is broken." I looked down at the scratched plastic watch on my wrist that had seen better years. Ol' Reliable.

11:47 am.

I was dumbfounded. I had only been in the woods for a half an hour. I was not gone for almost two hours. Was I? Perhaps my watch had broken, but Ol' Reliable never breaks.

Before Anderson could answer, Sparks and Bancroft marched over.

"Always in second, hey, Second?" Sparks taunted, smacking my arm. "Ooh, more ammo!" He scooped up armfuls of the green water balloons.

"Sparks, Bancroft, what time is it right now?" Anderson asked.

Sparks chucked a balloon at a passing cub. The boy squealed and darted in the other direction. "About ten-to-twelve, last I checked," the captain replied.

Bancroft grunted in agreement, replenishing Sparks's water balloon ammunition.

I couldn't believe it. No, I didn't believe it. I was only in the forest for thirty minutes max.

With nothing else to say, I replied, "Guess I got lost."

Sparks scoffed. "You? Get lost? You know these woods better than you've known any girl."

While normally Sparks's relationship analogies are directed towards his incompetence, I couldn't help but feel this one was accurate.

The last girl I thought I knew turned out to be a complete stranger.

The woods were more loving. They knew me, and I knew them. We understood each other. Leaves rustling on the trees, water rushing through the creek, animals scurrying along the path. My soul lingered in the forest. Everything I understood and could rely on— unlike anyone I had ever known.

But the girl in the woods felt different.

She felt like she was a part of the woods. That means in turn, a part of me.

Stop it, Second, I scolded myself. I rubbed my eyepatch. A constant reminder of *why* the forest was the only thing that knew me. The only thing I let know who the true me really was.

But deep down, a weird part of me hopes she will know me someday, too.

2:16 PM

A pang of guilt struck my stomach. It twisted every time I spoke to my cubs. My instruction was in the moment, but my mind was elsewhere. I needed to be all in, preparing these boys for a 6 day trip. I only gave my campers 50%.

The other 50% remained with her.

I can't stop thinking about her. I don't think it's love. That never works out, right? Those insta-love book or movie plots? The "love at first sight" and "happily ever afters" are lies to fuel hopeless romantics.

But now, I'm clinging to those lies.

Zipping my backpack, I instructed the boys that we were heading to our next activity: archery.

Seventy yards of fresh cut grass stood between the cubs and their targets. They lined up on the stone slab, bows at their sides and quivers on their backs. Anderson instructed his half of the campers. I did the same with mine.

But I was still distracted.

Was the mysterious Ghost Girl watching me? Could she hear me?

I finally pushed the thoughts aside and began the lesson.

Feet spread shoulder-width apart, I raised my bow. Setting an arrow, I pulled it back, resting my hand against my cheek. My left— and only—eye looked down the shaft, trying to focus on the target. It took every ounce of strength not to stare at the woods behind it. Exhaling, I released the arrow. It whistled and struck the yellow center.

"Arms up, Sweeney." I adjusted the boy's chubby hands, helping him grip the bow. Like all the other cubs, he's left-handed. I think I'm the only righty in our group. "With the proper form and some practice, you'll hit the mark every time."

Without a word, he nodded and fixed his posture. A bead of sweat dripped down his forehead. Taking a deep breath, he let go.

The arrow whistled through the air, striking the red ring around the bullseye.

A wide smile spread across Sweeney's face. He looked up at me for approval.

I smirked and patted his back. "Just like that. You're a natural." It made me proud to see improvement. But what made me truly happy was when the boys were proud of themselves.

Frankly, I wish I had that support growing up. A firm hand steering me in the right direction, a clap on the back when I did something well. Anything to prevent me from making mistakes. Someone to tell me right from wrong.

Any guidance at all, and I would still have both my eyes.

I shook my head hard. I needed my focus to be with the boys 100%. It was bad enough it stuck at 50% thanks to this Ghost Girl. I couldn't drop down to 25% because of my past.

"Captain Second," Cline called. He reached over his shoulder, trying to reach his quiver. "What does archery have to do with six days in the woods?" He tilted too far, and his arrows poured out, clattering to the ground.

Collecting his bundle, I half-joked, "If we run out of food, we'll be able to hunt."

"Hate to state the obvious, Captain Cyclops," Glover mocked, "but I think rock scrambling would be more helpful." He loosed his arrow, striking the bullseye.

I tried hard not to hate any child, but Glover irritated me.

I also keep calling them children. They're teenagers. Does that justify me hating him?

"Ooh, rock scrambling? I'm game!" Huerta exclaimed. He flicked the fletching on the arrow shaft. "If we scramble fast, can we get double dessert?"

"That's up to the chefs, not me," I replied. "But I might be able to arrange something." I sat down and slid my brown journal out of my backpack. "I'll think about writing a note to the chefs, but first you all have to put your equipment away." I waved my pen like a baton.

The boys grumbled and moaned but scurried around, tossing bows in bins and replacing arrows into their quivers.

One thing about these boys is when they want something, they work for it. I will try not to go easy on them this week.

A breeze just tickled the back of my neck. Goosebumps crawl over my forearms. I don't want to turn around. I might see her. I need to be present for these boys right now.

But if she keeps up, I think my distraction is going to get worse.

3:15 PM

One thing I'll say about my cubs: they're experienced. Despite their initial grumblings and complaints, they didn't disappoint.
Angered me? Sure. Disappointed me? Not quite.

After archery, all twelve cubs, Anderson, and I gathered our packs and raced to the edge of the forest. We weren't going up Mount Donwanago yet. Behind the survival area was a short but steep hiking route called Trail Smooth. The name is entirely misleading, but it was the perfect place to "train" for our trip.

"Be sure to keep up!" I called over my shoulder. I balled my fists and jogged up the hill with my cubs close behind.

At first, Trail Smooth's terrain was steady, clear, and easy to navigate. Deeper in, it grew steep and uneven. Trees had fallen across the path and boulders corroded into nature's staircases.

At the first scramble, I paused to look around. My eye followed a shimmer of light to my left. I stared for a moment, wondering—hoping—it was her. I wanted to see her soft round cheeks. Her long anti-gravity hair. Phantom or no, I couldn't deny she was attractive.

Glover snuck up next to me, startling me. "Cyclops, what are you staring at?"

I blinked hard. "Thought I saw something."

"How can you see anything?" He mocked. Gripping the boulder, he found his footing and started to climb.

Once again, I wanted to smack him. I refrained, though, because I would be fired if I didn't.

We scrambled up the first trail. It wasn't as steep as some of the paths on Mount Donwanago. The perfect warmup before tomorrow. I kept an eye on my six cubs. Sweeney lagged behind. It wasn't because he lacked athleticism as a bigger kid. It was because he kept getting distracted by taking candid instant-print photos. Leaves, trees, awkward cub poses. Thankfully, my brain got used to the flash after a while. As long as it didn't catch me off guard, I would be okay.

Cline and Pierce struggled the most out of my cubs, but Atkins stuck by them as support. They struggled together as a team. They showed the skill to toughen up and help one another out. Made me proud.

And Huerta? A little psychopath. He would race to the top, clamber back down, and then run back up again. He kept shouting, "Coffee power! Coffee power!"

Still ain't telling him it was decaf. If he has the energy, I won't stop him.

I do appreciate that they are a fun bunch (except for Glover). Some older teens are lame or "too cool" to listen to anyone. I know that from past experience at the camp and at home.

Sweat dripped down every limb by the time we reached the top. The stank of BO from fourteen guys caught in the wind. Our timing was above average for scrambling up Trail Smooth.

The boys are rather experienced. I have no doubts for our expedition tomorrow. An invisible weight lifted off my shoulders.

Heading out of the woods, we reached the first viewing point. It wasn't as breathtaking as the top of Mount Donwanago but still a beautiful spot. The forest stretched across the valley. A sea of green against the bright blue sky welcomed the sense of adventure. The air was crisp, the wind was cool. Picnic date worthy for sure.

Not that I have dates on the mind… I don't know what you're talking about.

"Who wants snacks?" Anderson called, pulling granola bars, fruit, and sandwiches out of his backpack.

The boys rushed to him like vultures to an animal carcass. They snatched the food out of his hand. Each found their own rock, plopped down, and munched away.

I took the opportunity to write in my journal—adding the time stamp of the start of our adventure.

As I wrote, Pierce—my cub that's rather quiet—came over and handed me a granola bar.

"Thank you, Pierce," I replied graciously. "Huerta didn't poison it, did he?"

He wiped his pointy nose. "He almost ate it, claiming coffee depletes calories."

"Oh, it sure does." I peeled away the wrapper. "At this rate, he'll lose five pounds by sundown."

Pierce smirked. "You know, you're not bad, Captain Second." Without another word, he turned and rejoined his friends.

A backhanded compliment, but a compliment nonetheless. I wanted the boys to warm up to me. Granted, it was only the second day. I already let them down once with Capture the Flag—whether they realized it or not. Relationships take time, and I hoped to care for ours a little better.

Anderson settled beside me, overlooking the valley. "How are you doing, dude?" He bit into a second granola bar–the kind that fell apart easily. The crumbs like sawdust tumbled into his lap. Delicious, but a trail would definitely be left behind.

"Good," I replied, half-heartedly. He didn't need to know what was really on my mind.

He grunted and swallowed. "Not convincing, but aight." He took another bite, and we watched the boys. "How do you think they're going to respond to our Campfire Chats starting tomorrow night?"

I shrugged. "I'm sure Huerta will be the one to break the ice. Atkins seems like a pretty open book, too."

My co-captain nodded. "Yeah, my guy, Weaver, seems chatty, too. I'll also share my story on night one."

"Do we want to end when we get to the top or when we get back to camp?"

Anderson took another bite. "Probably the top. I'd rather get to know them faster."

I nodded. These Campfire Chats were personal. A moment of forced openness between the cubs and captains. A way to get the guys to start talking about their feelings in a "safe space". Ugh, I hate that term. The amount of people who have said that to me to get me to open up about my eyepatch could fill a stadium.

I only half-looked forward to Campfire Chats. It warmed my heart when the boys opened up. Whether it was the truth or not was on them.

For example: I never opened up truthfully.

Sure, I told some twisted version of the truth. Even now, I lied to Anderson about being okay.

Water sloshed down my chin as I took a swig from my metal

bottle. Wiping my face with the back of my hand, I steered the conversation away from a depressing deep dive. "Well, Anderson, what are you doing after camp is over?"

He clicked his tongue. "Oh, man, I don't even want to think about going back. This place is serene."

As if on cue, Anderson's cub, Moss, ripped *brass* so loud I could've sworn the trees shook. Claps and chuckles erupted behind us.

Anderson and I couldn't help but laugh.

"Yeah, serene," I teased.

"Other than farts and horrible BO, I could honestly stay in the woods forever." Anderson took a deep breath. "I was so anxious about doing well and staying on time in college that I don't want time to exist anymore."

"They say time is a social construct sooo." I shrugged. "Make your own time."

A smile spread across my co-captain's face. "Maybe I will, Second. Maybe I'll take the time to hike the Vermont 5 like you did. I might not do it in a day, but I'll get it done before my new job starts."

"Do it, man. I don't regret it." Probably one of the only things I didn't regret. "What's your new job?"

"HR intern for an airline company." His nose crinkled. "It's not really what I wanted, but it gets me into the travel industry. I want to be a part of an international travel agency someday, so this is a start."

I clapped a hand on his back. "Good for you. It'll get you the experience you need. HR isn't easy, so good luck."

"Eh, if I can handle these guys," he jabbed a thumb over his shoulder, "I can handle anyone."

"I'll drink to that." I raised my water bottle.

Our conversation shifted from future aspirations to dumb jokes in the moment. We laughed and poked fun at the other campers. Don't get me wrong, I live for our stupid conversations about which kid looks the most like an actor we both hate or who could go the longest before going to the bathroom.

But that was it.

After talking about Anderson's future, we went back to talking about surface level stuff. The kind of chats employees have around the water cooler in an office. If anyone asked me any deep questions, I gave quick answers and didn't share anything further. It's just how it was. Guys don't talk about their feelings. No matter how insulted, confused, or sad, we held it in.

Well, I hold it in, anyway.

And I hate it.

5:35 PM

Finally: free period. I am happy to finally rest and unload the thoughts weighing down my brain. I need to unpack. I need to think.

I spoke to her today.

And I think I *blew* it.

After Anderson and I finished goofing around, we gathered the cubs and began our descent down Trail Smooth. A little more dangerous, but at least it was faster.

I tailed the back of the line, keeping an eye out as we scrambled down the rocks. Anderson led the boys in singing the Southpaw chant. A fun call and response similar to "Down by the Bay" where the last two lines are freestyle before restarting:

Down at Southpaw,
Where the Cubs all go
We learn new skills
To better grow
When we go home
We'll tell our friends…

"Have you ever seen a bear with no body hair?" Anderson sang as his last two lines.

"Down at Southpaw!" the boys yelled in unison.

This chant continued for the last hour of the trip. The boys started to get inappropriate with their rhymes, so we stopped the singing before reaching the edge of the woods.

"All right, guys, free time!" I announced, shooing them out of the forest.

They cheered, whooped, and raced to the center of the camp. During free period, they could relax, shower, play sports with the other guys, or have quiet time in prayer or thought.

"I'm probably gonna shower. I definitely reek," Anderson announced, running his fingers through his curly hair. "What are you gonna do before dinner?"

I shrugged. "Probably journal some more."

"You run out of pen ink yet?" Anderson teased.

"Not yet, but I'm getting there." I wagged my ballpoint pen at his face.

"If I see any lost pens, I'll grab 'em for ya." Anderson smirked. "If you're intending to share your journal as a memoir one day, be sure to make me look good."

I chuckled. "You're asking for a miracle."

He told me I was a *mama duck,* proceeded to flip me two birds, then ran off to the bathhouse.

Frankly, I needed a shower, too, but I finally had about an hour without responsibilities.

Turning around, I headed back into the woods.

I jogged along the same path I took when I saw the lights the first time. Bugs buzzed around my ears. Chipmunks scampered at my feet.

No sign of the lights.

I ran for about fifteen minutes—exhausted and doused in sweat again. Ready to give up, I decided to head back to the cabin. I took a shortcut, venturing off the path.

Halfway there, a murmur tickled my ear. Chills shot down my spine. I skidded to a stop and turned around.

A trail of lights sparked to life. They danced along the leaves, spinning and entangling around a thick trunk like rope to hang a hammock

Heart pounding, I followed them. My feet grew heavy with every step. The crunch of dry leaves quieted as if I walked along sand. At the edge of the lights, I looked up and stifled a gasp.

She was back. Perched upon a branch, the Ghost Girl tangled her fingers in her anti-gravity dress. Her transparent figure was paper white—from her hair to her dress to her eyes. She glowed like a star and floated like the sea. Whispers tumbled from her lips, but I could only catch a few phrases. It sounded like she recounted events or talked about her day.

My stomach knotted. I wanted to speak, but I didn't know what to say. I wanted to ask for her name or where she came from. Her beauty was captivating and I wanted to be her prisoner.

Three words she said aloud unraveled my heart: "I've been waiting."

I was convinced those words were for me. Why? I was unsure. But she waited for me.

Hands trembling, face flush, I took a deep breath. My voice floated up to her like leaves along the breeze. "You don't have to wait anymore."

The air stilled. Silence blanketed the forest. Her lips froze in place, forming a word that never came.

Beads of sweat formed on my brow. I prayed for her to say something. Anything.

Internally, I kicked myself. What cheesy, corny, psycho says "You don't have to wait anymore" to a girl who probably wasn't talking about you? Ugh, I hated myself more than usual at that moment.

I needed a save. I needed to tell her I was sorry. I didn't want her to leave.

I mustered up the courage to speak again: "I'm sorry, I don't know why I said that. I should have asked who it was you were waiting for."

Her head cocked to the side. Then, she spoke. "What is this?" Notes of fear, confusion, and awe strung along her voice.

"I am not sure," I replied, taking a step closer. "I've been hearing your voice over and over. Then, when I saw you…" I paused. "I had to say something."

A moment of silence hung between us before she asked, "You can see me?"

I looked up at her. Her head tilted downward, but she wasn't looking at me. I realized her white eyes had no irises.

The Ghost Girl was blind.

"Yes, I can see you, and I can hear you." I chuckled. "Can you see me?"

She shook her head. "Only your words."

Goosebumps raised along my arms. She couldn't see what I looked like. She couldn't see the past mistakes painted upon my face. The scars, the eyepatch, none of it.

She would only know me for the man I am now.

"That's amazing." I chuckled.

Her hand pressed against the tree trunk. It glowed beneath her touch. "What is your name?" she asked, leaning forward.

I stood beneath her tree. Her warm glow enveloped my body. My shoulders relaxed as I drank in her presence. It tasted of honey and the sweetest of flowers. "They call me Second," I replied. I didn't want to tell her my real name. My real name was associated with someone I didn't want to know anymore. I didn't want her to know him, either.

"Nickname, I presume." A smile spread across her face. "That's okay. I still don't understand what's going on. I've been doing this almost every day for years, but no one has ever replied to me."

"It's only because I didn't hear you until now." It sounded rude, so I quickly added, "But when you spoke to me for the first time, I haven't stopped thinking about you."

She giggled and it warmed my heart.

"I've thought of you every day for ten years," she confessed.

A lump caught in my throat. There had to be some mistake. I was sure of it. No one knew me that long. No one sought after me longer than they had to.

She must have been waiting for someone else, and I happened to stumble down her path.

In Sparks's story, he had mentioned that the murdered girl became a ghost, waiting for a man to love her and set her free…

No, that man was not me. She could not be the ghost in that story… Could she?

A trumpet resounded in the distance; the end of free time. She made no movement in reply. Perhaps she couldn't hear anything outside the forest.

I didn't want to leave. The forest trapped my soul, but camp beckoned my mind back. "I'm sorry to do this, but I need to go. I don't want to, but there are people who need me. Will you be back?"

Pushing herself up, she stood on the branch. The blood ran to my face as I scrambled back, not wanting to peer up her dress. I didn't want to be one of those guys. I stood behind a trunk and watched from afar.

"I haven't broken my routine in ten years," she said. She balanced her feet, one in front of the other. "The question is will *you* speak to me again?"

"Of course, I will." I tightened the straps on my backpack. "You may get sick of me by the end."

"How can I be sick of someone I don't know yet? You'll have to explain yourself when you return." She pressed the sides of her hands together. Her palms faced upward. "Until our next speaking, Second." She closed her hands as if in prayer.

Then, she vanished.

My heart still races after this encounter. I have no other words.

7:35 PM

Huerta threw a crumpled napkin ball at my head at dinner. "Captain Second, what are you thinking about that's more important than me right now?"

I was daydreaming, but I couldn't help it. I've been thinking about GG—short for Ghost Girl—ever since I got back. She took over my mind, but I welcomed the invasion.

"I've thought of you every day for ten years."

How can you say that to a guy and *not* expect him to think about it? What does it mean? Why has she been thinking about *me*? There was obviously some sort of mistake.

But she wanted to speak with me again… That was proof of *some* interest. Right?

I caught the second ball that soared across the table. "I'm thinking about all the stuff we need to pack before our trip tomorrow." I lied. I tossed the napkin back to him. "Are you ready for six days in the wilderness?"

"No duh, Captain Cyclops, that's why we're here." Glover spat. He picked apart his pancakes with two forks. Kinda violently.

Something about Glover irked me the wrong way. Not like he usually did with his insults. It seemed like something was on his mind, too.

I couldn't ask what was up. Not at that moment, anyway. Nor did I think he would tell me.

"The real question that no one is asking for some reason: what food are we taking on this trip?" Atkins announced, stealing Cline's breakfast sausage. "Lunch was pretty good today, but we can do better."

Cline tried to take back his property, but Atkins shoved it in his mouth before he succeeded.

Sweeney poked at his gluten-free toast and sighed, not saying a word. Instead, he pulled out his instant-print camera and took a photo of his pathetic dinner.

The kid barely spoke. Another cub I would need to connect with more on the hike.

I needed to refocus. The campers were my first priority. As a counselor at Camp Southpaw, I was in charge of the six boys' formation. If I wasn't present to help them, how would they grow?

"Let's make a menu right now," I said, pulling out my journal. Tearing a few pages out of the back, I scribbled down the boys' dream menu items for the next week.

As we discussed, Huerta tried to subtly pull my journal towards him. Pierce smacked his hand before I snapped at him. Huerta crossed his arms, huffed, and looked down at the floor.

So far, Pierce is my favorite. First he had given me a granola bar, then he proved he's got my back.

One boy down, five to go.

When we finished, Anderson and his six cubs joined our table. "Did you guys prep your half?" my co-captain asked.

"We outlined the menu." I handed him the sheet of paper. "Did you finish the packing list?"

He waved a little red notebook. "You're darn right we did."

One of Anderson's boys—Ortiz—covered half his mouth and whispered, "But we also stole some stuff."

I chuckled. "Are you making us accomplices?"

Sheepish grins covered Anderson and his Cubs' faces. "Not accomplices. Buyers," Anderson replied. He pulled a brown paper bag out of his backpack. "We're willing to offer you a deal."

"It's nothing illegal, is it?" Cline sounded genuinely concerned.

Ortiz took the bag from Anderson and opened it up for us to peer inside.

The scent of sugar and warm bread filled my nostrils. I didn't even need to see their glazy goodness to know exactly what they were:

Sticky buns.

No one makes Sticky Buns like Chef Jeff at Camp Southpaw. If they were ever low on donations, they could open a bakery solely for their sugary confection. They would be able to sell them so fast that the camp would be financially stable for three years.

My boys beamed, except for Sweeney. A frown stuck upon his face as he gazed upon the gluten-filled goodness.

"To *sweeten* the deal." Anderson gestured Madden to step forward.

In the cub's grip was a plastic bag filled with three sticky buns. The words "Gluten Free" scribbled onto the front.

Sweeney's face lit up like a beacon. His desperate eyes locked on me. It was very rare for the chefs to make the sticky buns—let alone gluten free ones.

I needed the boys to all trust me and like me by the end of the trip. I already won Pierce over. After helping Sweeney in archery, perhaps the sticky buns would be a tipping point.

I stood and held out my hand to Anderson who shook it firmly. "You've got yourself a deal," I said. "What do you want us to do?"

9:17 PM

We'd be cutting it close, but it was for the sticky buns. I would do *anything* for sticky buns. And for the approval of my cubs, but sticky buns first and foremost.

Apparently Sparks *glissed off* Anderson during free time. Something about teasing him about being afraid of ghosts. Knowing Anderson, it was not that big of a deal, but he wants to make a mountain out of a molehill.

If I get sticky buns, then I say let him be dramatic.

After we packed for our six-day expedition, we snuck across the camp grounds to accomplish Pack Cottontail mischief.

The plan was twofold: Captain Second and Cubs would invade Pack Coyote and take all of Sparks's clothing. After we've strung it to the flag pole and raised it, Captain Anderson and his cubs would execute their water-balloon sneak attack.

I wondered if Ghost Girl liked pranks. Would she approve of my mischief? I always hoped to find a partner-in-crime someday.

Stop it, Second. She's probably not even real. I don't know why I keep daydreaming.

Anyway, back to the prank.

Pressing a finger to my lips, I led my cubs alongside the cabins until we came upon Pack Coyote. I ordered Sweeney, Atkins, and Cline to keep watch while the rest of us snuck inside.

Their cabins were way neater than ours. All the beds were made, the bags tucked in their respective spots, and not a thing out of place.

I think Bancroft's love for order and organization rubbed off on Sparks and all twelve cubs.

The floorboards creaked beneath our feet. Sparks's bunk was in their second cabin on the far right. Unzipping his suitcase, I distributed the clothes amongst the campers. With armfuls of outfits, we raced back out of the cabin, across the campsite, and to the flagpole. We formed an assembly line to pass, clip, and hoist every article of Sparks's clothing up the flagpole.

As we attached the final sock to the rope, we heard a long shout in the distance:

"Andersonnn!"

"Go, go, go!" I yelled to the boys. We hoisted Sparks's clothing to the top of the flagpole and scattered in different directions.

Sweeney and Pierce followed me southeast past the Health Center. We stopped behind the building to catch our breath.

An array of laughter, shouts, and splashes echoed off the lake as the water balloon ambush ensued.

Peering around the building, I watched Pack Coyote battle it out with half of Pack Cottontail. Anderson almost ran out of balloons when the captains from Pack Marten and Bobcat rushed to his aid.

Waving to my other cubs, we ran out of hiding and joined the battle until we ran out of ammo.

Shredded balloons littered the campground like confetti. Everyone was wet in some capacity. Sparks was soaked to the bone. Ginger hair stuck to his forehead. His rust colored shirt clung to his thin frame.

He chuckled and extended a hand to Anderson. "I say we're even now."

Anderson shook it. "It'll teach you to mess with me."

Sparks wrung his shirt. A never-ending stream of water created a puddle of mud at his feet. "I don't think so, but it will prolong it." He sent his cubs to join Bancroft at the fire while he returned to the cabin to change, not knowing his clothes waved in the wind behind him.

The trumpet sounded and it was time for the end of night campfire. As we walked back, Anderson pulled out the two bags of sticky buns. "I say you upheld your end of the deal." He tossed them to me.

The treats weren't as warm as before, but that didn't matter. We won the grand prize.

When I held up the gluten-free treats, the biggest grin spread across Sweeney's round face. He pulled out his instant-print camera. I smiled as he snapped the photo, mentally ready for the flash of light. The memory rose from the top and he placed it in his pocket. Receiving his sticky buns, he spoke for the first time since introductions: "You're the best, Captain Second." He sank his teeth into one. Joy washed over him as he enjoyed his special snack.

I smiled. Another boy warmed up to me. Two down, four to go.

I passed the rest out, and each boy inhaled them.

"I can't wait to see how Captain Sparks reacts when he sees his clothes are gone." Huerta snorted, white glaze crusted around his lips.

Cline licked his fingers. "Will we get in trouble?"

I shrugged. "Possibly, but do we all agree it was worth it?"

All the boys nodded and enjoyed the last bites of their reward before taking their seats around the campfire.

Director Carter ended the second night with a testimony of faith. It was one he shared every year, so I took out my journal to document our adventure of the evening.

But my eyes kept darting to the woods. Honestly, I didn't want to tell my journal about my day anymore. I wanted to tell *her* how I heroically strung up my friend's underwear and raised them to fly over Camp Southpaw.

Would she find it funny? Did she have my sense of humor?

Halfway through the director's talk, a light flickered in the woods. I stared for a few moments to make sure they weren't just fireflies.

The butterflies in my stomach told me they were more than bugs.

I leaned over to Anderson and whispered, "I'll be right back. Watch my half, will ya?"

I'm going to stop this entry here. I'm praying she's in the forest. Is she waiting for me? Will I be able to talk to her twice in one day? Frankly, two times is not enough.

I don't know if it'll ever be enough.

9:56 PM

The lights danced around my feet as they guided me down a new path. They glowed so brightly I didn't need my flashlight. The butterflies flew frantically in my stomach as I entered the clearing.

Ghost Girl sat upon another branch, talking to herself again. She illuminated the forest; I wondered if anyone could see her through the trees.

Could anyone else see her at all? Was I the only one who knew she was here?

I sat on a trunk beneath her tree. My hands didn't know what to do so they passed the flashlight between them. I pinched my eyes shut and took a deep breath. I had never been so nervous talking to someone before. Would she even hear me again?

Wouldn't hurt to find out.

I looked up at her bright face. "Hey, I'm back."

She stopped whispering. A smile formed on her lips. "It's been a minute."

I cocked my head. "I spoke with you a few hours ago."

She counted on her fingers. "Nope. Days."

"Does time go faster for you?"

"Not sure, this is still weird for me," she replied.

"Same, but…" I paused, trying not to sound creepy. How could I tell her it was amazing and I wanted to know everything about her without sounding like a weirdo?

So all I said was: "It's kinda cool. "

She pressed her palms against the branch and leaned forward. "So, Second. What did you do in the time we were apart?"

I beamed. She said my name. She wanted to know what I was up to.

"I did a crazy prank for some sticky buns…"

Her lips formed an *o*. "Stop, that's hysterical. What did you do?"

I told her all about my cubs and my mischief. I explained elements of the camp. Finer details, not-important details, everything. How Camp Southpaw is backwards: breakfast for dinner, left-handed outweigh the right-handed, and everything is facing the outdoors.

Throughout our conversation, she'd smile. A few times I even made her laugh. Gah, her laugh. It became my favorite song. It was funny, innocent, and genuine wrapped in a single sound wave. Her giggle echoed across the forest and right through me. It found a home in my head and I didn't want it to leave.

After I talked about Camp Southpaw, she said, "Your job sounds like a lot of fun. The outdoors is more of my home than a house is thanks to my dad."

My eyes widened. "Your dad?"

She nodded. "He is a forest ranger. I've been outside since I knew how to walk. Bugs, dirt, none of it bothers me."

Sounded a lot like me, but I hoped she didn't suffer like I did.

Well… If she is the girl from Sparks's story, her ending was much worse than mine.

"Did anyone pick on you for being outdoorsy?" I asked.

"Eh," she raised her shoulders, "they think I stole my personality from a cartoon princess. Meanwhile, I've been an archer and nature lover since way before the movie came out."

"You're an archer?" I gasped. I jumped to my feet and moved closer to her tree. The lights illuminated the leaves crunching beneath my boots.

She nodded. White hair floated in front of her sightless eyes. "I have been since I was little. It's something my family and I can all do together."

Excitement bubbled inside me. "I'm not so bad at archery myself. Although, I'd rather be hiking or mountain climbing."

"You sound like a person I'd have fun with." Sweetness dripped from her words like honey, and I wanted to eat them up. She would have fun with me? She didn't even know me and she already thinks we would be compatible?

As friends, of course. Yes, I'm sure.

I shook my head hard. She's some sort of ghost girl. You're a stupid camp counselor, I reminded myself.

But the moments I was with her, I didn't want to believe it.

I cleared my throat. "So, is it okay if I ask for your name?"

She tapped the side of her face. "You can ask, but I'm not going to tell you. This mystery is more fun."

I didn't want her to know my real name, so I suppose it was fair. "Okay, but can I try and guess?"

GG smirked. "Sure, my real name starts with V. You only have three guesses."

V? Out of all the letters… I racked my brain trying to think of any female names that started with V. "Uh, Vanessa?"

She shook her head. "Nope."

I thought for about a minute, before I gave up. "I actually don't know any other *V* names. I feel really stupid right now."

She giggled. "Don't feel stupid, my name is pretty hard to guess—which is why I didn't mind you trying to figure it out."

"That hardly seems fair." I crossed my arms. "But I guess I can say the same about mine."

She arched an eyebrow. "Oh?"

"No, *M*. It starts with *M*. You have three guesses."

"Michael."

"Common guess. Nope."

She tilted her head back. "Okay, umm. Maxwell?"

I laughed. "One more guess."

She snapped her fingers. "Mark. Final answer."

I shrugged my shoulders. "Sorry, no prize for you."

"Ugh, now I know how it feels." She crossed her arms. "Maybe just change your name to Mark for me."

I shook my head. "Nope, too expensive."

GG laughed and leaned over her branch. "Fine, Captain Second. New question: will you tell me more about what you are like?"

Anxiety replaced my excitement. Should I tell her the man I hoped to be? Or the guy I was now? "Well, I don't know where to start."

"Is it you don't know where to start or you're afraid to tell me?" She smirked.

My heart jumped. She knew. How did she know? Could she hear it in my voice? Whatever it was, it made me want to tell her that much more.

Shouts and acclaims from the camp echoed between the trees. I ran out of time. I was only with her for a few minutes, but the real world passed by much faster.

"I'm sorry. I have to leave again." I apologized. My voice was heavy. I didn't want to go. I shook beneath her tree, gazing up at her. My heart told me to climb up and join her upon her perch. I wrapped my arms around the trunk of the tree. My body shook but the warmth that floated down was comforting.

But I had to get back to camp. The boys would get suspicious. Anderson would think I was crazy. I was acting irresponsible.

GG clicked her tongue. "It's okay, I've accepted you can't stay long during our visits. But this means you'll come back, right?"

"Absolutely."

She smiled and put her hands together as she did our last meeting. "Well, then. I'll talk to you later, Second." She clapped her hands and vanished.

I am lying in bed, writing by flashlight under the covers like a little boy up late reading his favorite comic. Her picture is vivid in my mind like a photograph I want to print and use as a bookmark of my journal. I want to learn so much more about her. Who is she? Does she know she's a ghost? Why has she spoken to me of all people?

She promised to come back, so I guess I'll have to wait for her.

August 5

DAY 1 OF THE HIKING TRIP

6:00 AM

The six-day trip was upon us. My mind did not want to focus. After last night, I could only think about GG. Her smile. Her *laugh*. How she said I'm the kind of person she'd want to hang out with.

The last girl who had said she wanted to hang out with me had an ulterior motive.

And it had cost me almost everything.

The boys didn't say anything about me ditching in the middle of campfire last night. It was as if nothing happened.

It was perfect. I was confident I could pull it off again tonight.

We awoke at 6:00 am. My six cubs had an easier time getting out of bed than Anderson's. That's because Huerta shoved all the kids off their cots to ensure we made it to the dining hall first. He wanted coffee before the trip.

We waited in line behind the serving counter for Anderson and his Cubs. The chefs were finishing breakfast preparations when we invaded. The scent of maple bacon and coffee beans floated through the hall. I let the aromas fill my lungs. I wondered if Ghost Girl's mouth would water like mine. Did she love breakfast as much as I did? Oh, crap, was she a vegan? I hoped not. I loved crispy crackling bacon, sweet sugary sticky buns, soft scrambled eggs.

My stomach growled. I pushed aside the thoughts and took a cup of coffee and a muffin. Huerta tried to snatch the mug out of my hand, but I held it above my head. "Uh no? Go get your own."

Huerta huffed and marched to the coffee station. As he turned to get his cup and lid, Chef Jeff swapped the pots. Jeff winked at me and went back to work. I smirked as my cub poured himself two cups—then two more—of decaf coffee.

Huerta chugged his fourth cup when the rest of our pack arrived.

"Are you ready for six wonderful days in the forest?" I greeted—half-sarcastically.

One of Anderson's cubs—Hart—groaned. "This is my least favorite part about camp."

"Which is funny because this makes up half of it." I chuckled, throwing my bag over my shoulder. "In case you all didn't know, it's expeditions like this that make my name known around here."

"That and being the only person named after a number." Glover snorted.

Anderson answered before I could think about strangling my cub. "Second is first when it comes to mountain climbing and hiking trips." He flung an arm around my back and pulled me in. "He is the only captain you'll meet who has hiked the Vermont 5 in one day. Anything we'll encounter, he's already done."

Atkins clapped. "Not bad, bro. I'm sure you've seen it all."

"No, he's only seen half of it," Glover grumbled.

I snickered. Glover may be a *brass*, but he's witty.

Huerta, however, had no composure and spat out his decaf. "'Half of it'? Aw *duck*, roasted!"

"Was that a coffee pun?" Cline asked.

"Keep all the terrible puns to a minimum," Anderson instructed. "Bad jokes are the captains' jobs." He patted my backpack. "And with Second and I at the helm, you'll have the best adventure ever."

I heard a zip as Anderson tried to steal the snacks I hid in the top pocket of my backpack. I spun out of his hold and pointed to the door. "Let's move out!"

This trip will be full of surprises, but I'll have to wait and see if they'll be good, bad, or both.

9:17 AM

Mount Donwanago matched its reputation for being the hardest hike at Camp Southpaw.

We were only about an hour into the hike when the boys began to complain. Their calves burned, they were hungry, they were tired, blah blah. Yeah, it was a workout, but you didn't hear me whine about it every five seconds. A few campers asked if I could carry their backpacks for them. I lobbed three over my back and climbed a few hundred feet just to prove I could. Then I threw them to the ground, saying carrying them further was against "company policy" so I couldn't.

Would Ghost Girl do a hike like this with me? Would she be able to keep up better than my cubs?

I stopped pinching myself by the fourth daydream. Then, I just kinda let them happen. I imagined Ghost Girl and I scrambling to the top of Mount Donwanago. The wind whisking her white hair behind her. A quiver of arrows on her back. The purest eyes looking out at the world at her feet. Then when she looks at me, she sees the person I hope to be for her. I cup her face with my hand. It's soft as I pull her in, my lips hovering over hers and—

"Ugh, Captain Anderson, can we stop?" Ortiz shouted.

Reality sucked me back from my daydream. It took a lot of willpower not to yell at a kid for whining about his "barking dogs".

I was grateful that my cubs did more than complain. Thanks to Huerta and the "coffee getting to him", the conversations picked up. He asked rapid fire questions to all fourteen of us.

"Last movie to make me cry?" I asked in response to Huerta's tenth question. I was thankful they were all stupid questions. Nothing too personal. "I think that animated movie with the house and balloons."

Not to my surprise, every boy whined, saying that movie had no business being that sad. I smiled to hear how many of them also cried during the five-minute opening montage. The main characters were friends who got married and only wanted to travel, but first, they spent their life together. Despite trials and tribulations, they stuck together.

Then when they finally had time to adventure, the wife passed on.

Now that I'm recapping it, it really was a depressing five-minutes. I was always told it was just me being over emotional. Guys aren't supposed to cry.

So, I tried not to. I withheld every tear and sad emotion throughout my life. No matter how broken and torn I was. No matter who tore me down and ripped my heart out. I didn't cry until it was too late.

1:03 PM

After the first scramble, we broke for lunch at about 1 pm. The view was the same height as Trail Smooth from the day before. Serene, peaceful, but not the best. The fresh scent of pine floated along the breeze. The sun beat down on my head as I sat beside Cline and Atkins, hoping to make conversation.

Atkins was a lacrosse jock whose parents pushed him to play in college. However, he claimed to be a "closet nerd". Obsessed mostly with aliens and the supernatural.

"Look, I love to play lacrosse, don't get me wrong," he reassured me. He crumpled his napkin. "People keep telling me I have potential to make it a career and get a full ride to college. But, I just don't feel it." He shrugged. "Is it so bad that I don't want to do the same things as my brother?"

I shook my head. "You want to be your own person, that's okay. Have you told your parents what you want to do?"

Shoving his garbage into his pack, he averted his gaze. "No, not yet. They're so excited about me joining my brother's college team someday, I haven't broken it to them yet."

I couldn't help but laugh. Not at him, but at his situation. I'd found myself in the same scenario long ago, but for very different reasons.

I was grateful Atkins only denied playing sports. Hopefully his parents and peers would be respectful of his decision. In high school, when I wanted to make a change, *she* made it impossible to do so without me being buried by guilt.

"Your parents sound like great folks for wanting you to succeed." I patted his back. "Don't be afraid to talk to them. They'll be more open than you think."

Atkins rubbed his hand through his black hair. "You think so?"

"I know so." I adjusted the baseball cap on my thick head of brown hair. "You're a smart kid, and they know that."

"I concur." Cline put in. Sinking his teeth into a sandwich, he added with a mouthful, "Your parents aren't the type you need to worry about. They just aren't sure what you like to do."

Atkins cocked his head. "How do you know that?"

"Our parents talked at drop off the other day." He swallowed. "I heard them say that you didn't seem happy about the next school year, but you looked forward to this."

A grin spread across Atkin's face. "Thanks, Cline. Thanks, Captain. I'll try to talk to them."

I patted his back. "Hey, if you ever need advice even after camp, reach out to me. The real world can be tough, and I'll do what I can to help." I jerked my chin toward Cline. "You too, little guy."

The two beamed and thanked me.

"I've seen the other captains here at Southpaw and, I have to say, you and Anderson are pretty cool," Atkins stated. "Also, I know some people think it's weird you have an eyepatch, but I think it's kinda sick."

"Yeah, like do you have an epic battle story?" Cline asked with wide eyes.

"Ooh yeah!" Atkins rubbed his thick jaw. "And with the beard? You look like the kind of guy who has literally fought other pirates."

My face fell and I chuckled nervously. I wished it was an epic battle story. Day after day, the voice inside me reminds me it's my fault. I was too emotional. Too fragile.

Well, that's what I was told, anyway.

"It's not that impressive." I zipped my backpack. "I'll be sharing a story at one of our last Campfire Chats." That's all I would share. A story. They didn't need to know if it was the truth or not.

The two cocked their heads. "Campfire Chats?" Atkins asked.

"Basically the talk we had right now." I pointed between us. "We would ask you to share with the class."

"Like free therapy?" The joy in Cline's voice worried me a bit.

I nodded. "Like free therapy. So I expect you both to be open. Let's get the other boys comfortable enough to talk with us."

The two nodded, and then I excused myself to go check on the other cubs.

Four down, two to go.

I didn't think winning the boys over would be so easy. Perhaps I misjudged them.

Plopping beside Anderson, I let out a long sigh. "How are you doing, dude?"

"Good," he said, swatting the crumbs off his shirt. "You seemed quite chipper this morning."

"Am I not chipper every morning?"

He snorted. "Definitely not. Did you have a nice dream about someone special?" He elbowed me.

I rolled my eye. "I didn't dream which made me sleep more soundly."

"Uh huh." He turned and yelled at one of his Cubs to stop peeing off the side of the mountain before continuing our conversation. "Is there a new lady in your life? I heard through the grapevine that the last one was a glitch."

The question took me aback. I didn't blink for a few seconds. No one was supposed to know about her. I did my best to separate my past from the camp. It was supposed to be the only place I was safe. Free. Memories were not allowed to haunt me here. I didn't want to think about her. About her contorted face covered in blood…

"Dude, you look like you've seen a ghost," Anderson teased. "We barely talk about our personal lives, so I thought I'd ask."

He wasn't wrong. We've been co-captains for years and consider each other friends but didn't hang out much outside of camp. I shook my head hard, pushing away any thoughts of the past. "Why, do you have someone you could introduce me to?"

Anderson's sarcastic laugh echoed down the cliff side. "Dude, I was praying you had someone you could introduce me to."

"How can this," I waved a hand at his face, "not find any girls?"

"Oh, sure, my perfect skin and cheekbones gets me plenty of girls." He winked. "Just not the one I really want."

I bit my tongue. I tried not to scold him for being too picky—if he was being serious. If he knew how hard it was to find a girl who wasn't afraid of his face, he wouldn't be saying anything.

Then again, he must think something of me to ask if I knew anyone. Either that or he knows I face rejection on a regular basis.

I needed to stop. Anderson saw through the eyepatch. He was a friend. Someone I trusted. I couldn't think so low of him.

"Nah, haven't met anyone worth talking about yet." I averted my gaze. Of course there was a girl worth talking about. But to say that I may be developing feelings for a girl in the forest who is probably a ghost? Not normal. He would think I was insane.

"Eh, that's all right." Anderson's back cracked as he stood. "We'll find our people some day." An open hand offered to help me to my feet.

I took it. "You're right." Flinging my backpack over my shoulder, I called to the boys to get ready to continue.

"We should hang out sometime after camp," Anderson suggested. His tone was genuine. No malice or ulterior motive detected.

"If we're not too far away, I think we should," I replied. A hint of wariness hung on my words. People getting close to me never ended well for either party.

Well, then why do you want to get close to ghost girl? a voice inside me asked.

Jaw clenched, I shook the thought away. She was different. She wasn't real. I couldn't hurt her. The only way she can hurt me is by not showing up. I had to prepare myself for that.

But I'm used to being hurt.

7:35 PM

We didn't stop until it was time to settle in for the night. The start of this entry is stamped at about 7:35pm. I feel like I won't have much time to write in my journals during the day.

That's okay. It's only the night that matters. When I can process my thoughts. When I can see her without anyone noticing I'm gone.

The fire crackled in the center of our circle. The scent of spices, smoke, and chicken filled my nostrils. Over an open flame, I made the cubs trail chili. One of my specialties. Chicken, beans, rice, cheese, and mild spices (too hot would result in a digestive disaster).

I handed out the bowls to Anderson's cubs first. Hart, Madden, Moss, Ortiz, and Weaver. I repeated their names, trying to recount them all. I really only had to pay close attention to my half, but I should know everyone.

As I handed out portions to my own cubs, my eye darted deep into the wood. The setting sun cast long shadows between the trees. Red-orange light dripped from the green leaves like paint.

"Yo, Captain Second." Huerta whistled, shaking his metal bowl. "You gonna hook a brother up?"

Refocusing my brain, I plopped dinner into his bowl. "How's the coffee feeling?"

Huerta held his forehead. "Giving me a migraine since it's out of my system. I need more."

"Drink more water," I shouted as he left for his seat.

Sweeney sat next to me with his instant-print camera. His eyes cast downward. "Captain Second?"

"No gluten in this one, Sweeney." I handed him a bowl. "Is chili okay?"

He nodded and took it quickly. "It's not the chili." He fiddled with the camera in his hands. "Is it okay if I take your picture? You were okay with the sticky bun photo last night, but I think I need to ask you for permission first. I'm sorry, I didn't know you didn't like your picture taken."

Sweeney thought I was camera-shy. I'm not; I actually love my photo taken. Clever angles not showing my face are preferred, but I'm pretty confident. It's when bright lights catch me off guard… "Of course you can take my photo, Sweeney. Just let me know so I can be ready for the flash."

A grin spread across his face. "Yes, of course!" He peered into the viewfinder and gave a countdown. I posed as he snapped the photo.

Even though I was prepared for the flash, a phantom pain spread across my chest and the memory pricked my mind:

Lights.

Glass.

Si—

I shook my head hard. It was not fair. I wanted to create new memories but bad ones resurfaced. I shoved the thoughts back and finished scooping Sweeney's dinner.

When the photo printed, the cub nodded, grabbed his bowl, and sat back on his seat.

Glover fetched his food last. He snatched it from my hand. Hot chili sloshing onto my wrist. I cursed under my breath and flung off the hot remnants.

"Language, Captain Second," Anderson teased. The boys chuckled.

Huerta shoveled the last bit of chili into his mouth. After a pathetic burp, he said, "You know what this campfire needs?"

"Marshmallows?" Fischer asked.

"Yes, but also no." Huerta jumped up and tossed his bowl to Pierce who dropped it. "It needs a ghost story."

Atkins clapped. "Yes, bring it on!"

"Ugh, but we already heard one from Sparks," Hart whined.

Huerta paused. "Well, I really hoped you liked that one because it's the only one I know."

"Before we get into your retelling," Anderson said. He rubbed his hands together. "Why don't we all settle down for our first Campfire Chat, okay?"

"Which is what?" Glover snapped.

Cline licked the back of his spoon. "Free therapy."

"Eh, close enough," I said. "It's a chance for us to get to know each other. We talk a little personal and here you can ask for advice or encouragement. Basically it's like that cheap purple gym: a judgment free zone."

"So, you want us to talk about our feelings?" Glover snorted. "Is this a girl's slumber party?"

"No, it's a man-to-man chat," I retorted. "No need to be afraid to share."

"Oh, I'm an over-sharer," Huerta announced. "I have no issue going first if it helps."

"Can someone else go first, please," Hart complained. "I think he's shared enough."

"Hey, whose pack are you a part of?" Huerta rolled up his hoodie sleeves dramatically. He's seen too many movies.

"Why don't you go tomorrow, Huerta." I jerked my chin toward Anderson. "Captain Anderson will go first and then two more. We'll do about two-to-three a night until everyone has had a chance."

None of the boys objected further.

"Great, I'll start." Anderson cleared his throat, and waved. "Hello, everyone, I'm Captain Anderson."

"Hi, Anderson," half the boys said in unison.

"I'm twenty-three and fresh out of college. Camp is something I do for fun, but honestly, it's because I love to boss people around."

The cubs laughed.

"It's true, though!" Anderson protested. "I love making schedules and plans. Being on time is important to me."

"Is that why you yelled at Madden this morning for taking too long of a *tish*?" Moss snorted.

Anderson shrugged. "Perhaps. It's a habit of mine that's hard to break. When I was in high school, I put so much pressure on myself in order to become the best. It was a lot to handle, but I never saw progress." He reached into his shirt and pulled out a string with a smooth stone dangling from it. "Then, an odd one-eyed friend told me something about four years ago"

Huerta smiled and pointed to me as if it wasn't obvious.

Anderson chuckled. "He claims he doesn't remember this, but he said, 'Isn't it crazy that this stone was put under rushing waters for years before it became smooth?'"

"Yeah, it's a *rock*." Glover rolled his eyes.

"Exactly." Anderson turned the rock over in his hand. "Rocks are under pressure all the time, yet we still think they're cool. This rock was attacked by a ducking river for years before it became smooth and well rounded." He put the necklace back inside his white shirt. "I realized that stressing out in one day wasn't going to do anything. Rather, I needed to be patient and let the stress of life smooth me out. I won't see the results until I'm finished."

I snapped my fingers repeatedly and the boys joined in the quiet applause. I had heard Anderson's story before. It still shocks me every time. I had never realized the impact such a simple line had on him. The boys didn't know that we had been bathing naked in the river with Sparks and Bancroft, flinging mud at one another after a long hike. That would take away from the profoundness of the message.

"That's actually kind of helpful." Weaver chimed in. The boy proceeded to vent about issues with classes. At first, the other cubs appeared disinterested. Then, they engaged in conversation that relieved a few campers' troubled minds.

The smiling, laughing cubs reminded me why we had these Campfire Chats. Words needed to get off their chests. Stresses they didn't tell their parents about. They knew they were safe within the forest.

"Now, can I re-tell the ghost story?" Huerta whined.

A gust of wind rushed through the camp. I thought I was the only one to feel it, but Atkins and I locked eyes.

A smile spread across the cub's face. "Dude, that was freaky." Atkins laughed.

"Captain Cyclops, break out the marshmallows." Huerta jumped up. "That's a sign from God that I'm meant to tell this story."

I pulled the squishy-white treats out of my bag. "Fine, go ahead. But we need to go to sleep soon, so either break it into chapters or tell it quick." I never would've stopped him. I wanted to hear Sparks's story again. It gave me an excuse to think about Ghost Girl and maybe understand *why* she is trapped in the forest.

Huerta cleared his throat and stood over the fire. In a poor attempt at a haunting voice, he began, "'Three wrong words break a heart. Five wrong words consume a soul. Ten wrong words last eternity.'"

"That's not what he said," Madden protested.

"Yes, it is!" Huerta snapped. "I have a great memory."

"Captain Second can be the judge of that," Pierce said, pointing his roasting stick at me. "Did you write down his story in your journal?"

"Not the whole thing." I lied. I pulled out the torn leather book and thumbed through the pages. I found the entry from around 9:00 pm last night. I smirked. "Huerta got it right."

"Thank you!" Huerta threw his arms out. "Now, let me continue." He cleared his throat. "So, there was this girl about the same age as Captain Second and Anderson." He held a marshmallow between his fingers. "She was sweet, small, and squishy like this marshmallow."

"I can attest that Captain Sparks did *not* say that," I interjected.

"It's a *retelling!*" Huerta shouted. Placing a hand on his chest, he coughed and continued, "She loved her friends. She was super fun and smart. Basically, she could be the CEO of a brand-new fancy company. But," he crushed the marshmallow in his palm, "someone didn't want her to. Someone mean, nasty, and evil. Someone who had the kind of search history that would have given Grandma a heart attack. He was basically a complete and total *brass*-hole. Someone who did not deserve the sweet marshmallow." Huerta uncurled his crushed treat and popped it into his mouth.

"I appreciate how you're giving more depth to Captain Sparks's original story," Cline put in. Chocolate smeared around his lips. "Although Captain Sparks's story was more chilling."

"Hey, I can make it chilling!" Huerta wiped sticky fingers on his pajama pants.

"Can you sleep on it and tell us more tomorrow?" Pierce yawned. "I'm about to pass out."

"I mean we did walk ten miles today," I added. I sandwiched three pieces of chocolate and a marshmallow between two graham crackers. "We're stuck with one another for a while. You have a captive audience." I sank my teeth into my treat. The sweetness melted in my mouth, coating my tongue. Sticky white marshmallows stretched between my fingertips as I swallowed the last bite.

Huerta growled. "Fine, I'll separate the story into chapters. I'll tell you more tomorrow." He dropped into a stance and dragged his finger slowly across the air. "But ye shall hear the *entire* story, as told by D. Huerta."

"We're looking forward to it," I said. Tossing another log onto the fire, I watched the embers crackle and the sparks shoot upward. They tangled and danced high into the night sky. I sat back and watched them float into the forest.

My heart stopped in my chest.

In the distance, a white figure passed behind the trees. A quiet murmur tickled my ears.

Then, she vanished.

I shook my head and faced the boys again, acting as if nothing ever happened. We chatted for a while before they settled in. One by one, they began to drift off while I wrote in my journal. I killed time patiently waiting until I could sneak away.

I just pray she's still wandering in the forest.

10:32 PM

Euphoria. Noun. A feeling or state of intense excitement and happiness.

That doesn't even come close to how I felt when I was with Ghost Girl. It's going to be the death of me.

Crickets sang as I snuck away from our campsite. It didn't take long for the boys to fall asleep. No one would notice the bundle of blankets resting in my hammock wasn't me. I thought I felt someone watching me, but I'm sure they assumed I left to take a *tish*.

I looked down at my watch. 10:32 pm. I had a few hours to spend alone with her—and I couldn't wait.

Embers flickered to life between the trees. They waited for me. Lights danced excitedly as I approached, eager to lead me to her.

Pine and lavender filled my lungs. I floated along the scent like in a dream until I stood beneath her tree.

Words fell from her perfect lips like water down a mountain. Their sound could soothe any worried soul.

"I hope I didn't keep you waiting too long," I said confidently. I wanted her to know I wasn't afraid.

Her chant stopped and she smiled. "It makes it that much sweeter when you return."

I craned my neck to watch her, wondering how I could get closer. "You barely know me, but you look forward to my visits?" I was one to talk, though. I had thought about her all day.

"You left me on a cliffhanger last time," she teased. "You have to tell me what you're like."

Oh, right. I would talk about almost anything else. I wondered if I could lie to her? Perhaps tell her about a man I thought she would want to see?

No. I was done lying. I needed to learn from my past mistakes—especially in relationships.

"As you know, I love the outdoors—like you." I gestured to her. "In fact, I'm pretty well known around here for my feat of hiking the Vermont 5 in one day."

She nodded and said, "Not to stroke your ego, but that is rather impressive."

"Yeah, I'm just *that* good." I picked up a stone, turning it over in my hands.

"Did you hike them on your own or with a group?" She swung her legs back and forth. "Were you scared?"

I threw the rock. It bounced off a tree trunk, landing with a *plop* into a puddle. I had to think about my answer. I had hiked alone because it was during a time I hated everyone. Had I been scared? No, I had been angry. Frustrated. I had hiked five 4,000 foot-tall peaks in one day because I had not been able to sleep. I had practically run up those mountains trying to escape past frustrations.

Had it helped? I'm cooler now, that's for sure. I hid behind the mask of this new reputation. No one needed to know what I hiked away *from*.

But I couldn't tell her any of that. "Did it alone," I said. "Not really scared, just tired afterwards." I wasn't going to lie to her, but I wasn't going to tell her the whole truth either. I needed to be honest with GG as much as possible, but she didn't need to know every detail.

She smirked. "I believe that! The Vermont 5 are high peaks. Does that mean you're from Vermont?"

I shook my head. "No, I live a bit further south."

"Not gonna tell me where?"

"Not yet, we're still strangers," I teased. "I don't want you knowing where I live. You might try to kidnap me."

She giggled. *Gah*, a song I could listen to on repeat.

"Fine, then let's stop being strangers!" She scooted closer to the tree trunk. "How about life stuff? What do you do outside of camp?"

The question of the century. "I just graduated college with a degree in general education and a minor in creative writing. That was my life the past few years, so I'm not quite sure what I want to do now."

"Understandable." She wrapped her arms around the tree. "Do you have any inkling as to what you want? Job or otherwise?"

My parents kept asking me that question. If I could, I'd be assistant director at this camp during the summer, write self-help books in the winter, and speak in schools in the spring.

What I really want is to save boys from the pains of the outside world. I'd teach these Cubs what it took to be men—and what it really means. I don't want anyone to make the mistakes I did.

But that was a dream I was told I couldn't accomplish.

I shrugged. She didn't need to know all of that, either. "Kind of, but I don't think it's feasible." Not a lie.

GG pressed her body against the trunk. With a slow exhale, she jumped. She descended like a leaf fluttering to the ground. Her bare feet touched the grass beneath her. A warm glow spread out from her toes, igniting the darkness of the woods. It wasn't a quick flash that brought up painful memories. It was a sunrise that warmed my soul.

She stood in front of me. Her warmth kissed my cheeks. My heart wanted to pop out of my chest and jump into her embrace.

"How do you know it's not feasible until you try?" she asked.

Because everyone stopped me, I thought. "You're right." I felt like I withheld so much of who I am, but I didn't want to scare her on our first date.

Wait, stop it, Second. Not a date. Not a date.

"Good, because your job needs to make you happy, otherwise why do it?" She swayed back and forth like a little girl twirling in a new dress.

Her adorable mannerisms distracted me; I almost missed what she said. I cleared my throat. "You're right. I'll think about it more."

She nodded. "As you should. Now, what about your appearance?"

"My appearance?" I asked sheepishly. I hated describing myself. I didn't want her to know about the mistakes scrawled across my face.

"Yes, please describe it," she pleaded. A smile spread across her glowing cheeks as she took a step closer.

Her dimples awoke the butterflies in my stomach. "W-well," I began. I combed my fingers through my thick hair—not that she could see it. Confidence. I needed confidence. "I'm a brunette. I have a beard, otherwise I look like I'm twelve."

She giggled again and my heart melted.

"I'm a six-foot tall white boy, but I tan like a true Italian." I rotated my arms and flexed. "I wouldn't say I'm a gym junkie, but I take care of myself."

"Gotta take care of yourself," she reiterated. "Now what about the rest of your face? You say you minored in creative writing, so describe in detail."

My cheeks burned. "Uhh, well." I paused.

"No lying, I want to know!" she chirped. Her translucent body hovered closer to me. "What does your face look like?"

I took a deep breath. She was most likely a ghost hiding in the woods of Camp Southpaw. Who was she going to tell? "Well, you know I have a beard. Couple freckles here and there. My nose? Uh, arrow shaped. Not quite Roman, but I have a little bump." She thought too highly of my descriptive abilities.

"And your eyes?" she prodded.

I sucked in a deep breath. No lying, I reminded myself. I whispered, "It's blue." Not a lie, but not the whole truth.

She cocked her head; her hair floated around her cheeks. "'It's'? Does that mean something else?"

My ears burned. She read between the lines. Ghost Girl saw through me—even though she was blind.

"I wear an eyepatch over the other." I stroked the leather. It burned my fingertips. "It shouldn't have happened. I was out with someone when they—"

The memories flickered behind the eyepatch.

Lights.

Gla—

No. No. I wouldn't let it happen while I was with her. The present belonged to her. The past was gone.

I exhaled, and confessed, "I lost it a few years ago."

She moved closer. Closer. Closer. The air between us grew thick with warmth like a soft blanket. Her scent of lavender and pine enveloped me. Fingers hovered a few inches from my face. I wanted her to touch me. To press her hand against my cheek. I prayed for the heat radiating from her to melt away the memories frozen in my mind.

"How? What did they do? Who did that to you?" She breathed.

The butterflies' party in my stomach was out of control. They fluttered and flapped, tingling all four limbs. All I wanted to think about was Ghost Girl. I didn't want to recall any miserable moment of my past. I wanted to lean into her palm and kiss it sweetly. To thank her for worrying about me. She wanted to know about my pain. She wanted to know why I was hurting.

No one had asked me that before.

A lump caught in my throat. "She is long gone." I forced the words out. "I'm convinced I did it to myself."

The girl made a fist and backed away. "The pain you feel is justified," she whispered. "Sharing pain with someone who understands is the first step to mending a heart."

A lump caught in my throat. Why does she understand? Why would a beautiful girl like her know something like what I've been through?

She let out a quiet sigh. "Well, I understand if you don't want to open up yet. We're still strangers after all." She smiled. "I won't press you."

I wanted her to. I wanted her to beg me to tell her. To wonder what girl tore me apart, destroying me physically and mentally.

But guys aren't supposed to talk about their feelings. I changed the subject: "I've talked about myself for a bit. It's your turn."

She turned away from me. "I guess if we have to," she joked. Glancing over her shoulder, she asked, "What do you want to know?"

Everything. I needed to know her favorite color, movie, food, time of day. What got her out of bed in the morning, what makes her laugh, how I can help her if she cried.

"Uh, I guess how old are you?" I refrained from punching myself in the face for asking a stupid simple question.

"I'll be twenty-three in September," she said. "I'm guessing you're about twenty-one?"

I shook my head. "I'm older than you. I was held back from college after my accident." The words poured out before I could suck them back in.

Thankfully, she didn't press further. "That makes me feel better. I don't want to be a cougar."

I laughed. "I think I'd have to be a young camper's age for you to be classified as a cougar."

She rolled her eyes. "It was a joke, Second." She stuck her tongue out.

I bit my lip. Her childish response sent my heart racing. My hormones flew. I wanted to be closer to her. *Carp*, I was falling further and further for a ghost.

"I-I promise, I'm good at jokes." I stammered. That was a poorly constructed sentence. "I mean, I have a good sense of humor. Sarcasm is a love language of mine."

"Glad we have that in common." A moment passed before she covered her mouth with her hand. "Oh boy, I'm fading fast." She yawned. Sadness filled her eyes. "I'm so sorry, Second, but it's my turn to run away from you."

I wished she'd stay. I wanted her to tell me everything. But I couldn't. I had no control over her, and I accepted that.

"As long as you come running back?" The last word rose in tone.

"Like I said, I've been doing this for years." She put her hands palm up. "It's you who finally showed up." With a wink, she said, "Have a good night, Captain Second." She clapped her hands.

Darkness blanketed the forest. Her scent faded. Murky humid air replaced the comforting warmth.

I closed my eye as I clicked on my flashlight. When I opened it, I stared at where her feet touched the earth. My watch read 1:50 am. It only felt like an hour. It wasn't long enough. I stood and waited, hoping she'd say "Just kidding" and come back. My heart called out to her, but she didn't reply.

Stop it, Second, I scolded myself. But it is too late. I am pulled out by the tide. Nothing could bring me back to shore.

A Captain goes with his ship, and Ghost Girl is mine.

August 6

DAY 2 OF THE HIKING TRIP

6:35 AM

This morning I awoke with a skip in my step and a smile on my face as Director Carter would say… Basically, an overly complicated way of saying I was hyper. Despite only four hours of sleep, energy shot through my limbs like I downed four energy drinks. I was ready to go and get the day over with. I yearned for the night so I could be alone with her.

I beat a spatula against a metal pot. "Rise and shine, cubs. Gotta eat so we can get to scrambling!"

The boys groaned and hid under their sleeping bags.

"Captain Second, it's too early," Atkins grumbled.

I stoked the fire I sat behind. Bacon crackled in the wide pan. Its salty scent wafted along the morning breeze. "It's never too early for a good day."

"He's right, even though it's annoying." Anderson yawned. He plopped down on a stump and poured a cup of instant coffee.

Huerta rolled across the grass in his sleeping bag. "Is that coffee I smell?"

I leaned over and whispered, "Don't let Huerta have the good stuff."

My co-captain winked and poured the last drop into my flask.

"You can only have some if you get all the boys up and ready," I promised.

While Huerta jumped up and executed his mission, Anderson and I finished making breakfast. Trail egg sandwiches aren't quite the same as an Italian deli's, but they're pretty good. Bacon, egg whites, and cheese stuck between a roll. How could you go wrong?

I cooked Sweeney's separately so there was no cross contamination. The boy's eyes smiled as he took his share. He placed it on the ground, arranged the leaves around it, and snapped a photo. He took the undeveloped image and placed it with the rest.

Huerta ran up with a coffee cup in each hand. "Hand over yer booty, Captain," he ordered in his best pirate-voice.

"Aye, aye." I shook my head and poured him two cups of decaf.

When Huerta went off to gulp down his treasure, Anderson elbowed me. "Your cubs seem to really like you. I'm struggling with mine." He jerked his chin toward two boys that sat quietly against a tree. "Some won't even speak to me."

"Just force yourself into the conversation and keep doing it until they reply." I sipped my coffee. It was bitter without any sugar, but the nutty tones were spot on. "That's what I do, anyway."

"And if that doesn't work?"

I shrugged. "I'll let you know when I figure that out. I think Huerta is almost entirely on my side, but," I jerked my head towards Glover, "he is the tough one."

Glover sat on his backpack eating breakfast. His eyes remained fixated on a line of ants heading to their hill. Different emotions crossed his face. Sadness, frustration, curiosity.

"I guess we'll both have to wait it out." Anderson clapped my back. "Now, finish breakfast! We've got a big mountain to scramble."

The boys cheered, but Glover's gaze wandered from the forest and landed on me. A shudder shot through me.

Something is not right. He worries me, and I'm not sure why, but I'm determined to find out.

12:09 PM

I am *this close* to losing my *tish*. We didn't even get to the scrambling part yet. We broke for lunch early because the boys whined. Anderson's half needs some discipline.

Hart whined and groaned, dragging his feet through the dirt. "Captains, please, if we don't stop now I will die."

The crest of the hill was nowhere in sight. There were not many places to rest. But the complaints from the cubs made me want to tear my hair out. I even carried two of their bags so they'd shut up. "Okay, fine, we'll make a stop for lunch. Make it quick." I tossed the extra packs onto the ground.

The boys rejoiced and found random rocks to perch upon. Thick trees lined the footpath to our left. A cliff bordered our right. On one side you'd get lost easily, the other you'd tumble to your death. Not the ideal picnic spot.

"Everyone stay close," Anderson ordered, unzipping his backpack.

I sat down and pulled out my sandwich. My ballpoint pen slipped out of my bag. I swore as it clattered down the rock trail. It flipped like a high-diver as it plummeted off the cliff side.

Pierce watched it tumble down. He whistled. "Uh oh, that's not good, Captain Second."

I exhaled, trying not to get frustrated. That was my only pen. The thought of not being able to journal almost sent me to panic. I *needed* to document everything—especially Ghost Girl. I needed to ensure I remembered every detail. "That was my only pen," I grumbled.

Pierce dug through the pocket of his backpack. He pulled out a ballpoint pen and a brand new pencil. He extended his arm. "Take these, Captain. I have plenty."

"Are you sure, Pierce?"

He nodded. "I always bring extra in case I get inspired to draw."

I took them and carefully zipped them in the inner pocket of my bag. "Thanks, dude. I really appreciate it."

The cub smiled. "I know the pain of losing an art tool."

"Pierce is good at art," Huerta said with his mouth full. "But he keeps refusing to draw my portrait."

"When you can pay or trade me for something, then I will," Pierce replied.

"You know I have no money." Huerta took a swig of water. "If I did, I would buy a drawing of me in every outfit I own."

"Is that three drawings then?" Glover mocked.

He looked down at his filthy t-shirt. Come to think of it, he had worn the same shirt yesterday and the day before. I assumed he was just filthy. Glover alluded to the fact that he didn't have any other outfits...

"Why, yes, Glover," Huerta joked, holding up three fingers. "This outfit, my pajamas, and my birthday suit."

Pierce cringed. "I don't need that image, man."

Before Huerta could go on about being drawn in the nude, I redirected the conversation. "How long have you been doing art, Pierce?"

"The past few years." He pulled out a sketchbook. Black-inked doodles stretched across the white cover. Its rings bent from use. "Nothing too traditional. It's a hobby. I haven't done it much during camp because I don't want my sketchbook to get dirty."

"Might I suggest wrapping it in your socks or underpants?" Cline butted in. "The weather looks like rain today."

I gazed up at the sky. The nerd was right. Dark clouds circled the sun, threatening to block out its light. The air grew cooler since we sat down.

"Maybe not my underwear, but I'll keep it safe," Pierce replied, replacing the book in his bag.

Atkins tore a piece of beef jerky between his teeth. "Captain Second, why do you write so much in your journal, anyway?" he asked, chewing obnoxiously.

"I was a creative writing major," I replied. "Practice makes progress, so I try and do it every day." Not a lie, but not the whole reason. My therapist prescribed journaling to document my life. He claimed it would aid in expressing emotions and keep events clear as they occurred. Basically a way of saying "have evidence for when you get manipulated again."

"What do you write about?" Huerta prodded.

"Oh, embarrassing things about you, Huerta." Sarcasm dripped from every word. "I wrote down all the secrets you spilled in your sleep."

All the cubs laughed. Well, all of them except Glover. He glared at me as he bit into his granola bar. A hidden warning hung in his dark eyes. I didn't know what to make of it.

"As long as my name is in there, I'm happy." Huerta jumped up. "If you publish your journal into an autobiography, I want the world to know my name."

Glover scoffed. "No one would want to read *his* story."

Heat bloomed in my cheeks. I tried so hard to not let Glover get to me. I don't know how I am going to get him to like me by the end of the session. It is clear he hates me. And, frankly, I am not a huge fan of him either.

"That's not true, Glover." Huerta hopped over to him. "I'm sure we'd all read it to see my claim to fame." He clasped a hand on Glover's shoulder.

Glover's eyes widened. He sucked in a breath through gritted teeth. In a swift motion, he swiped Huerta's forearm, shoving him off. Huerta tumbled backward. Twigs snapped like cracking bones beneath his weight.

"Hey!" I jumped up. "That was unnecessary."

"Don't touch me," Glover snarled. "Ever."

Huerta raised his arms. "Chillax, *amigo*. I didn't mean anything by it."

Pierce rose and pulled Huerta to his feet.

"Don't shove each other around on a mountainside," Anderson scolded. "Especially not when it's raining."

I held out my hand. The gentlest raindrop plopped on my calloused palm. The sporadic rain cooled my hot skin. I hoped it'd remain light. "Quickly finish up so we can get moving," I told them. I inhaled the last bites of my sandwich and pulled out my journal to document with my new pen.

As I wrote, I felt Glover's eyes pierce the side of my head. He knew something; it irked me that I didn't know what it was.

I hope his hatred for me won't escalate, but something inside me says it will only get worse.

4:04 PM

Rain drizzled from gray clouds as we hiked. The rocks' color darkened as we clambered up the next trail. The droplets remained light and steady, but we knew worse was coming. We quickened our pace to head to our next campsite. The path had grown steeper. By around 4 pm, we made it to the most challenging scramble of the day.

I stayed at the bottom of the pack, watching the cubs follow Anderson to the top. It was a Class 2 rock scramble. Moderate terrain. Less footholds, steeper inclines, and higher heights. A little unnerving to be in charge of twelve kids.

The worst part? The rain poured in the middle of our ascent. The forest darkened and dread flooded our spirits. The boys' bodies shook as they slowly climbed.

"Gah, Captain Anderson, I don't like this," Hart cried. Wet bangs clung to his eyelashes.

"We have to keep going," my co-captain ordered. A mist erupted from his lips when he spat. "We're almost there. It'll be safer at the top."

My heart thumped loud in my ears as the drops beat against my forehead. I focused my eye on the rocks in front of me. I gripped each stone as hard as I could, hoisting myself up. I could probably have scrambled up it in a few minutes, but I wouldn't abandon the boys. I remained behind them as the caboose.

Anderson, Hart, and Fischer reached the top of the cliff first. They hoisted themselves up and over with grunts and joyful exclaims.

A gust of wind ran around the side of the mountain. A few Cubs squealed and clung to the mountainside. Atkins's foot slipped, loosening a rock. It tumbled down and clipped my shoulder.

I sucked in a breath between gritted teeth. "It's okay, readjust your footing and keep going!" I shouted. "Only way to go is up."

"Or down if we let go!" Huerta called. He hastened his pace and ascended. He made it safely.

Cold rain shot down faster and faster. Dark clouds circled the sky. One by one, almost all of the campers reached the top.

Pierce was the last camper to make his way upward. He

outstretched his hand to pull himself up.

A clap of thunder shook the mountain.

Startled, Pierce lost his grip. A gasp erupted from his lungs. Arms flailed, trying to grab Anderson's hand. He missed. A scream echoed off the mountain as he slid down the cliff side.

Pierce's body hurled toward me, kicking up rock and dust. He clawed at the rocks in a desperate attempt to regain his grip.

I planted my feet and extended my right arm. His body crashed into me and we slid down together. The air shot out of my lungs and my heart thumped hard in my chest. Every muscle tightened and ached, but I didn't let go. We dug our feet into the mountain.

Our fall stopped halfway down. Panting heavily, I clung to the wall with Pierce under my arm. Mud splattered against our cheeks. "Are you okay?" I panted.

Tears streamed down Pierce's cheeks as he nodded.

"It's all right. I'm not going to let you go." I promised.

The roaring wind made the cubs' shouts inaudible. The storm circled above us. I prayed for its departure. I prayed for the strength to keep him safe. My body ached as I shielded him against the elements.

A long rope dropped down the side of the mountain until it dangled between us.

"Second, what do we do?" Pierce panicked. "My hands hurt." Thick red dripped from the boy's palms.

Blood.

My heartbeat quickened and a lump caught in my throat. I buried my panic as best I could. "They're probably just scratched. We'll clean them when we get up there."

He jerked his chin toward me. "Yours, too."

I glanced over to see red trailing down my wrist. I hadn't felt it. I wished I hadn't seen it.

My eye burned and the skin behind my eyepatch tingled. That horrible night shoved its way to the front of my brain. My senses overstimulated. The past and present danced before my eye. Memories wove in and out of my vision.

The storm wind became sirens.

Pierce's sobs, my tears.

The boy's shouts, her curses.

The blood, everywhere.

I pinched my eye shut and sucked in several breaths through my teeth. The visions faded slowly.

"Second, are you okay?" Pierce's voice shook.

I sucked in a few more breaths until my mind returned to the present. I shook my head hard and attempted to ignore everything but Pierce and his safety. "Yes. Now, let's tie this around you." Pressing my elbow against his back, I grabbed the rope. Precariously I passed it in front of him until it was clipped tightly beneath his arms.

"Wait, don't let me go," he begged. His puffy eyes widened.

"It will be okay." I looked up at Anderson who nodded. Then, I slid my hand away.

Pierce clutched the rope with his bleeding hands. The boys above us shouted and pulled him up.

As he ascended, a blink of light caught my eye. My heart hammered as the painful memories tried to resurface. I shook my head and looked closer.

Between the raindrops, the Ghost Girl's figure flickered from the treetop below me, leaves hiding her from the boys above. Her wide eyes remained straight ahead. She couldn't see me dangling precariously from a cliff side.

I sucked in a gasp. "What are you doing back so soon?" I said aloud. That was the first time she appeared next to me. The first time she sought me out—somehow. I was honored but it really wasn't a good time.

"I keep thinking about you," she whispered through the woods. Her quiet voice cut through the shouts of the cubs and the screams of the rain. The rushing wind silenced around us. Everything stilled. My life threatening situation felt like a friendly chat. "I wanted to talk to you and see if you were okay." Tears welled in the corners of her white eyes.

My heart beat loud in my ears. Was something wrong? Why did she want to check on me? "I'm currently dangling from the mountain right now."

Fear crept across her face. "Purposefully, I hope?"

"Nope, but I'm okay. A little cut up, but okay."

She gasped. "Oh no, oh no, I'm sorry. I hope I didn't cause you to fall."

I fell for her differently, but that was no time for flirting. My fingers cramped as I clutched the rocks. I looked up, waiting for the rope to drop. It took them forever. My body wanted to give up. I could collapse to the ground. Best case scenario is I lost a limb. I could live with that, right?

No. I needed to hold on. Burning shot through my muscles. Everything ached. After a moment, I finally replied to GG, "No, a camper slipped. It's pouring rain."

"Oh no… I'm praying for you." As the words fell from her lips, the lights dancing around her fluttered to where I dangled. Their glow heated my hands.

I tried not to freak out as the sparks encircled my wrists. The burning in my fingers disappeared. Strength returned to my hands. Adrenaline coursed faster down my limbs. I felt like I could climb Mount Everest. "I-I appreciate your prayers," I replied, dumbfounded as the lights faded around me.

"I won't bother you anymore." Her tone was apologetic. "Please focus on saving yourself."

"*Pfft*, you're never a bother. Don't worry, Anderson is going to pull me up soon. I'll be fine. It'll take more than this to kill me." It was true. I could be dangling from the side of a mountain and I would welcome her company.

Which I was. I wonder if that says anything about my feelings for her…

A small smile spread across her face. My body warmed in the chilling rain.

"Thank you, Second." She wiped her eyes. "It means more than you could know."

I cocked my head to the side. Before I could ask her to elaborate, the rope hit me on the head. I looked up to tug on it with my right hand. When I glanced back at the woods, she was gone.

I cursed under my breath as I wrapped the rope around myself. I tugged it three times, and the boys hoisted me up.

Anderson grabbed my belt and threw me on my face. All the boys cheered and clapped when I was finally safe.

Propping myself on my elbows, I looked up to where Pierce sat in front of me. "Are you okay?"

He rubbed his eyes with his sleeve. Bandages wrapped around his wrists. "Yes, thank you."

Cline and Atkins ran over with the first aid kit. They took my hand and wiped the dirt away. Their eyes widened.

"Pierce? Thought you said there was blood," Atkins stated.

"There was." I turned my hand over.

My palm was cut-free.

Heart racing, I quickly added, "Bandage it anyway, it may have washed off in the rain."

As they wrapped my palm, I felt a glare from Glover cut through me. I wished I could read minds; it would make understanding him so much easier.

Anderson brushed his wet curly bangs out of his face. "We should set up camp early and take shelter until the storm passes."

Pierce's body trembled. "Please, I need a minute."

Anderson nodded. "Okay, but be careful under the trees if there is lightning." He extended a hand to me, a kind look in his eye.

My lips formed a straight line. Anderson was my friend, I always needed to remember that. I took his hand, and he pulled me to my feet.

"Captain Second, please document this quickly so we have the details of the incident in case parents come suing." Anderson joked.

"We signed waivers so if we died out here they wouldn't care," Glover grumbled.

Cline's eyes widened. "No, that's not true unless I missed the fine print."

The boys argued over the waivers their parents signed while I scribbled my entry, trying to shield my journal from the rain.

My heart beats faster in my chest as I look down at my uncut hand. How did she do that? But more importantly, why does she think she's a burden? I won't let that question go unanswered.

6:57 PM

We spent the rest of the evening waiting out the storm. When none of the cubs wanted to press forward, we settled in for the night.

The mishap wore me out—which is a light way of putting it. Despite my exhaustion, my mind raced faster than a car in the Indy 500. My thoughts went in circles until they'd eventually cause my brain to go up in flames.

The events of the day left the boys exhausted. Almost watching a camper break a limb sliding down a mountain will do a number on anyone.

I absentmindedly poked at my wet wood fire while Anderson set up tents with the boys. The flames crackled as they battled the slow dripping rain. The downpour had ceased, but the damp chill rattled our bones.

Pierce sat beside me with a blanket around his quaking shoulders. A tear dripped down his pointy nose. He sniffled and wiped it with his sleeve.

"How are you holding up?" I asked.

Pierce pulled his hood tighter around his head. "I can't believe that happened," he whispered. "I dunno if I can scramble another mountain."

I placed a hand on his back. The hand that should have throbbed. The hand that should have been wrapped in a blood soaked bandage if it wasn't for Ghost Girl—somehow. "Don't say that. You're a skilled hiker," I said sincerely. "Those conditions were dangerous. We should have sought shelter, but the heavy rain happened so fast."

Pierce shuddered. "I feel like I'll be anxious until the end of the trip."

"Oh, I'm always anxious," Hart said. Five logs slid off his arms, plopping into the mud beside my fire. "I just learn to move in the rhythm of my anxiety."

Pierce tilted his head. "How do you manage it?"

"Wait, hold up," Huerta butted in. "Is this the start of Campfire Chats? Because you said I could share tonight."

I shrugged. "I mean, I guess if—"

"Everyone gather round!" Huerta shouted, louder than necessary. "Everyone needs to pay attention to Hart and Pierce and then to *me*." He dramatically flipped his greasy dark hair.

"You're lucky we're all done setting up," Anderson said with a laugh. "If the other boys are fine with it, we can begin our evening routine."

"Shouldn't we wait until dinner is served?" Hart asked nervously. "I mean, I don't mind sharing, but—"

"I want to go, so you have to go *now*." Huerta slapped his leg. "Captain Second can make dinner while we chat."

I rattled the pots obnoxiously as I pulled them from the bag. "Why of course, your majesty. I'm at your beck and call."

"Isn't that your job anyway?" Glover snorted. He sat beside Sweeney, his cold eyes locked on my miraculously healed hand.

Atkins chuckled. "Lay off him, man, and just be happy to eat." He patted Glover's back.

The cub swung around and smacked Atkins's hand. "Don't. Touch. Me." Glover growled. Brown eyes glowed red with rage.

Atkins put his hands up. "My bad, dude." He crossed the campsite to sit beside Madden.

"Enough of this." Huerta clapped twice. "Campfire Chats have begun. Hart, continue. You were talking about moving with your anxiety?"

"O-oh, yeah." The *swish* of Hart's jacket zipper as he repeatedly played with it fell in rhythm with his words. He spoke of normal situations that morphed into struggles in his mind.

"I've accepted that there are things I can't control," Hart said. "My brain will still think of every scenario. I will still be nervous, but," he shrugged, "I focus on the outcome that I want, not the one that I think will happen. It's harder than it sounds, but it's made me happier."

"Like the outcome of this hiking trip?" Pierce sniffled.

Hart nodded. "The worst case scenarios always play out in my head." He flicked his jacket zipper. "Like how we could get struck by lightning and die tonight. However, the best case scenario? We sleep soundly and wake up tomorrow. So that's the one I'm going to focus on."

"That's how I feel when I draw sometimes," Pierce added. "I just doodle and scribble until I find an idea I want to focus on. Something that makes me happy."

Hart clapped. "Exactly! Think of that, and you won't worry about falling off a cliff even if you're on flat ground."

Anderson snapped his fingers in applause, and the boys copied. Quiet snaps entangled with the crackling sound of the flames.

Before anyone could take a breath, Huerta blurted, "Is it my turn now?"

Anderson closed his eyes and groaned. "Yes, Huerta."

The cub jumped up. "Excellent." He cleared his throat. "Hi, everyone, call me Huerta."

"We know who you are, just get on with it!" Glover snapped.

Huerta threw his hands up. "Relax. I just wanted to say I'm happy to be here. My house can be sad sometimes, so I wanted to say thanks for making my summer super happy and fun. I like to tell stories that make people smile."

"Your ghost story retelling ain't really a fun fairytale," Madden mocked.

"That one is an exception." Huerta stuck a finger into the air. "And it is one that I will continue to tell."

"Does it make you happy to tell it?" I asked, stirring peas, carrots, and beef into my pot of rice.

A grin spread across Huerta's face. "It sure does."

"Then keep your happiness and continue telling us the Ghost Story." I exclaimed, pointing my wooden spoon. I desired only the best for all these boys. While Huerta's Campfire Chat was brief, a dark sorrow hung between the words. In the silence screamed a cry for joy. For acceptance.

"Can we get our food first?" Fischer—Anderson's quietest cub— asked. His long fingers pressed against his growling stomach.

"Nope, eat while I tell it," Huerta exclaimed. "I'll serve you. Dinner and a show." Taking a wooden bowl in each hand, he waited for me to fill them with stir-fry before he started, "Yesterday, we talked about the mean evil man who wanted to hurt the girl who was as sweet as a marshmallow."

"Dude, no more food analogies." Madden's request came out as a bitter command. "I'm starving."

Huerta shoved a bowl into the cub's chest. "Food is coming!"

"Hey, no fighting!" Anderson snapped. He rose to help distribute dinner. "Huerta, continue."

The boy shook his head. "Nope. I'll wait then." Pain welled in Huerta's eyes. A familiar sad expression I wished he did not show.

I scooped the last bit of rice into my own bowl. "Huerta, can you share what the man did to the girl? Why was he mean?" I pushed aside the vegetables and ate a spoonful of rice and beef. The salty flavors warmed my mouth.

Huerta shook his head hard. Once. Twice, then his expression flipped. Brightness returned to his eyes. A smile spread across his cheeks as if each shake reset his brain to return to the happy Huerta he acted out to be. "The man was toxic." Serious notes danced along his words. "He manipulated her. Saying she wasn't good enough. Not smart enough. Not pretty enough. He made her feel stupid in front of everyone."

My stomach twisted as I thought of her ghostly face. Her smooth translucent skin. Anti-gravity hair of a mermaid. Everything about her was beautiful. What distorted lens covered the man's vision when he looked at her?

"Then, one day." Huerta held up his spoon. "She decided she'd had enough." He slashed the utensil like a sword across his body. "It was time she fought back. But who proved stronger?" He shrugged. "That will wait until tomorrow."

"You complained all day about telling us the story to just tell us that little bit?" Madden scoffed.

"She's a ghost who's literally been waiting forever for someone to save her." Atkins shoveled the last bit of rice into his mouth, and then said with bulging cheeks, "We can wait one night."

Except I couldn't. I waited all day. I waited all evening.

I have so many questions for Ghost Girl. As soon as the boys fall asleep, I will find her.

But will I be the one to save her?

11:58 PM

Moonlight cut through thick clouds, blanketing the campsite in a blue glow. It was almost midnight when I snuck out to find Ghost Girl. The boys took a bit to fall asleep. I struggled to keep my eyes open as I lay wrapped like a caterpillar in my sleeping bag.

I peeled back the covers and slid out of my hammock. My boots stuck into the mud with a quiet *schlup*. I froze for a few moments, waiting for the stirring campers to settle. As I snuck away from camp, I felt two eyes stuck on my back. I prayed if anyone saw me, they would think I went to take a leak. Hopefully that would make sense to them and they'd drift back into sleep.

Raindrops drizzled from the dark sky. I pulled the hood of my jacket tighter around my face. A sneeze tickled my nostrils. I scrunched my nose, holding it in. I failed.

A third sneeze threatened to wake a bear when the lights finally appeared. Their warmth cut through the damp. Pine and lavender overpowered my senses. I ran to be at the lights' center, soaking in their glow. It heated my heart. I ventured to her spot where she sat waiting for me again.

"It's my turn to ask questions now," I blurted. I wanted to change up the conversation. We talked of me, me, me. I wanted to hear about *her*. I know she is an archer who loves the outdoors. She also thinks I'm the kind of person she'd like to hang out with, but that wasn't enough. I needed to know everything.

Most importantly, I needed to know who she was and how I could help her escape the forest.

Frankly, that should have been my first question, but she was a mystery I wanted to solve. I wanted to unravel her story and take it piece by piece, cherishing every small detail like a treasure. I wouldn't take anything for granted.

The corners of her mouth turned upward. "Ask away, Second."

She said my name, and I was done for. Speechless. All eloquent articulation flew from my mind like a bird leaving the nest. What could I ask her? *How* could I ask her? Did she know she might be a ghost? What was ghost-etiquette? Could I say, "Are you dead" and not offend her?

I had no idea, so I asked, "Tell me what your life is like." A neutral request.

She clicked her tongue. "That's not a question, nor did you say please."

I removed my hood and stepped closer to her tree. "Please," I pleaded.

"Fine." She brushed her anti-gravity hair behind one side of her neck. "Other than waiting for you? I wake up, go to work, take care of my family and friends, go to sleep, repeat."

I assumed her memory must've been stuck in her past life. I am no ghost enthusiast like Atkins, but perhaps that's a thing?

I hugged the tree. My heart pounded in my ears as I pondered my next move. Might be stupid, but I wanted to do it anyway. "Do you enjoy what you do for work?"

She nodded. "I do, actually. I am a huge planner and my job requires me to keep things neat and organized."

Wrapping my legs around the trunk, I hoisted myself up a few feet. "Sticking to a plan or checking off a list is so satisfying." I kept my voice steady as I ascended.

Eyes wide, she blurted, "Yes! Thank you! Some people don't get it. My sisters for sure."

Sweat and raindrops slid down my temple as I pulled my body further up the tree. "How many sisters do you have?"

"Four, and they're a handful." She wrung her dress. "We don't always see eye to eye."

"You can't take it to heart. I have one little sister and we fight all the time. But she still loves me." My shirt tore and bark scratched my bare skin as I scooted further up. I didn't care. I wanted to be next to her. I needed to taste the lavender and pine. I needed to drink every last bit of light she exuded.

GG nodded. "I know, I know. It's hard sometimes."

I reached up and grabbed her branch. The wood was dry. Pulling myself up, I lay across the limb.

Her heat penetrated my wet clothes, drying them in seconds. Rain fell around us. It slid off of an invisible umbrella enveloping GG and me. The world quieted until the only sound was my heartbeat. Magical. Invigorating.

More questions stuck on the tip of my tongue, but I hesitated. I needed to get something off my chest. "I forgot to tell you. Thank you for saving my life earlier today."

She cocked her head; she wasn't facing my direction. "Today?"

I looked down at my watch: it stuck to 11:58 pm. The same as before I had left. "Oh right, time is different." I pushed myself upright sitting with the branch between my legs. "When you told me you didn't want to bother me. You being there actually saved me."

Sparks fluttered around her eyes. It crackled and popped like electricity.

It awoke the butterflies in my stomach.

"I didn't really do anything," she confessed. "But I'm glad to help."

I needed to be closer to her. I wanted to feel her voltage. I wanted it to electrocute me until I reduced to ash. "You did, but I have one more thing to ask." I scooted along the branch. "Why did you think you were a bother?"

She bit her lip. "I hate annoying people." Sadness singed the edge of her words. "I don't like to seem like a burden."

A lump formed in my throat. *Burden.* That word tasted like a disgusting food you were force fed as a kid. Like broccoli. But worse.

"Why would you be a burden?" A foot kept us apart. I extended a hand, ready to brush her cheek. Touch her hair. Let her know I was here. That I was real.

And I needed *her* to be real.

She leaned backward, my hand missing her shoulder. My heart hammered as she pulled away. Did she do that purposefully? Could she sense me reaching for her?

Her sightless eyes locked on the ground. "Can you ask me other fun questions first? Before we go into the sad stuff?"

I swallowed the lump in my throat. Whoever made her feel like a burden hurt her. They tore her apart.

I wanted to put her back together.

"Oh, uh, sure. Let's talk fun stuff." I rubbed my hand through my hair. "How about food? Do you have a favorite?"

A smile spread across her cheeks. "These are the kind of questions I love." Ghost Girl rose to her feet, walking down the limb like a gymnast on a tight-rope. "French fries, hands down. Give me a salty potato and I'll eat ten of them."

I chuckled. "Junk food? You're speaking my language. Although, I'm a sweet guy, myself."

She glanced over her shoulder. "You seem sweet."

Red burned my cheeks. Butterflies fluttered in my stomach. She was so *ducking* cute.

Ghost Girl laughed. "Do you like to adventure, Second?" she asked.

"Absolutely." I wouldn't have been talking to a ghost if I didn't love adventures.

"Are you adventuring now?"

Yes, and you're my greatest adventure. Is what cheesy-writer-me wanted to say. I am not good with emotions out loud, so I replied, "Yep."

Her dress hovered like a satin sheet swaying in the wind. It shimmered and shined in the moonlight. As I watched, I felt trapped in a photograph I never wanted to forget. A memory I wanted to cherish forever, no matter how faded the edges became.

Extending her arms, she jumped from the tree.

I gasped and shot an arm out, trying to snatch her dress as it plummeted to the ground.

But she didn't fall. She floated like a leaf in autumn. Light spider-webbed out from where her feet kissed the earth. The trees' roots drank it up and their leaves glimmered and glowed. Sparkles shimmered along the forest like a thousand fireflies.

Awestruck, my wide eyes took in every detail. Heaven sent its angel to bring the stars down to earth. GG blessed the woods with her beauty and grace.

Whoa, Second, relax, man. Your descriptions are getting worse with every line.

Anyway.

I forced myself to speak: "What do you consider an adventure?" I scooted back towards the trunk and clambered down to the ground.

Ghost Girl spun as she thought. Sparkles flickered off the edges of her dress. "The wind in my hair, doing something different. Something fun. Feeling like there are no problems in the world. Just me and the person I'm adventuring with."

I hopped off the tree. "You prefer not to adventure alone?"

She nodded. "Adventuring alone is boring, isn't it?"

"You have a point." I rubbed the dirt off my palms. "Who do you adventure with?"

"No one as cool as you, that's for sure." She turned and made her way down the path.

Quickly, I chased after her. Everything she said made my heart sing. A few kind words combatted the hundreds of hateful curses and slurs someone embedded into my mind. "You're pretty cool too," I admitted. "I'd love to adventure with you more sometime."

We walked in silence for a moment. Her arms swung gently at her sides. I wanted to reach out and take her hand; to feel her warmth and comfort. But I refrained.

High green grass took over the further we went, narrowing our way. Raindrops beat around us, but we remained dry.

She paused and wiggled her fingers. Her bright hair glimmered. "If we're having an adventure right now, can you describe it to me?"

I put one foot up on a stump. "Describe it?"

"You said you loved to write, so think of it as a creative prose exercise." She spun around. "And you know I can't see." White eyes glowed like the moon.

The butterflies in my stomach freaked out. Her gaze captured me. I froze, waiting for her to set me free, but I didn't think she ever would.

"Okay, I'll do my best." I cleared my throat. "I'm better at describing on paper than out loud."

"Aww, are you nervous?" she teased.

Thankfully, she couldn't see my face redden. "No," I lied. "I need a moment to gather my bearings." My eye darted between the trees, quickly taking in my surroundings.

Something magic or electric hung in the air as she waited for me to speak. It pricked my lips, and the words spilled out.

"Darkness blankets the forest. It isn't frightening nor unnerving. It's heavy and warm like a sleeping bag by a fire." I kneeled down and dragged my fingers through the dirt. "A cool earth sleeps beneath our feet. Soft dirt awaits the morning when critters will scurry across it." Tilting my head, I listened. "The crickets sing their lullaby. Harmonious chirps weave between the trees. Every once in a while, an owl accents their song like a cymbal crash." I inhaled deeply. "Evergreen trees wave in the breeze. The air tastes like Christmas." I stood up and faced Ghost Girl. The butterflies in my stomach sent out a warning. "And at the center of it all glows a beautiful—" I stopped.

"A beautiful what?" Her soft tone cut through the forest.

I wanted to finish my sentence. I wanted to describe her beauty and how I felt warm, safe, and yet captive with her.

But I listened to the butterflies' warning… and lied: "I meant at the center of it all *grows* a beautiful oak. Its branches reached towards the glimmering stars. Reaching for a place where it doesn't have to worry. Where it's free."

"I envy the tree," she whispered. "Second, that description was beautiful. I feel like I'm really with you." A soft smile spread across her cheeks. "You truly are talented."

I rubbed my palms nervously. I struggled to accept compliments. "Ah, I'm all right. Still learning and practicing my craft."

"Oh, just take the compliment!" She flicked her wrist. "I know the feeling of not being able to accept them. It's tough sometimes. Even tougher when you don't receive them much, so that's why I'm giving more than I get."

I tilted my head. My mind returned to our previous conversation. The sadness in her words when she asked to change subjects. "Is that why you feel like a burden?" I reached out, praying for the bravery to touch her cheek. To feel her warmth and to give something back.

A long sigh floated from her lips. "Maybe. I don't know. I just feel like I am. There is someone in my life that always makes me feel terrible even if he doesn't know it."

My hand jerked back. She said he. Maybe her dad? Or her brother? Wait, no brother; she said she only had sisters. Maybe her boss?

I rubbed the back of my neck. "Uh, who is he?"

Sadness hung in her eyes. "My boyfriend."

The butterflies scattered and my heart shattered. My lips failed to form words. Was it a coincidence that a Ghost Girl appeared in the woods after Sparks told his story. She talks about a ghost boyfriend who treats her like a burden...

Was Sparks's story true?

Stunned silence overtook me as I stood in thought.

Her brow knotted. "Second, are you still there?"

"Yeah, yeah, sorry." I didn't know what to say. Just a moment before I wanted to reach out and touch her. To feel her warmth beneath my fingertips. But now I feel like I've been burned. Harmed by a story I didn't want to be real. A story that ended in hatred, betrayal, and murder.

My stomach twisted. If the Ghost Girl is from Sparks's story, the boyfriend she talked about in present tense will *kill* her in the future.

"Sorry to dump all that on you." Her voice was small and timid. "I just feel like I don't have anyone to talk to about him."

Hope flickered. The way she spoke of him meant we were in the middle of her story. She is stuck right where Huerta ended his re-telling a few hours prior. Perhaps there was time to save her.

"You can talk to me about anything."

She gave me a small smile. "Thank you, Second. I just worry about him finding out from someone other than myself."

My chance to ask who she was. I shrugged and said, "I don't even know who you are, so I doubt I'll be able to say anything." My heart pounded in my chest as I waited for her reply.

She bit her lip. "Maybe it's safer to keep it that way for now."

My pounding heart caught in my throat. I blew it. I thought I was smooth, but this damn boyfriend of hers scared her into keeping it a secret.

I swallowed hard. Why was I so worked up? Why was I so upset? She's a ghost. She's probably not even real.

No.

She *was* real at one point. And in some life she felt like a bother to a guy who should've taken care of her. A guy who should have treated her like the treasure that she was. A guy who should have loved her.

But instead, he took everything from her.

I glanced down at the hand she had healed. She saved me. Maybe it's my job to help her. For her sake and mine.

At the end of Sparks's story, he had said that Ghost Girl waited for a man to love her as she ought to be loved. *"One man struck her down in the forest, now she waits for another man to pick her up."*

I decided it is *my job* to love her and send her home.

I will heal her heart and break her murderer's curse.

I inhaled deeply through my nose. I wanted my voice to sound confident. Strong. "When you're ready to tell me your name, you let me know. For now, know that I will do whatever I can to help."

Her glossy eyes shook. "Why? I've only spoken to you a few times."

"Because you feel like a bother and you are far from it. Any time he makes you feel like that, you come to me. I will be waiting for you."

Tears magnified the light in her cheeks. "Thank you, Second. I hope to repay you someday." She put her hands side-by-side. "Thank you for our little adventure, today. I hope to have more with you soon." She closed her palms and vanished.

Rain battered down on my head; the sounds of the forest resumed. I stood in the center of the woods, pondering. My feelings for GG were a seed and she was the sunlight. They were growing fast, but I don't know what they'll turn into.

All I know now is I will be waiting for her to let me into her life.

Like I wished someone had done for me.

August 7

DAY 3 OF THE HIKING TRIP

6:45 AM

I am impatient. GG has been waiting for who knows how long and I can't sit still for five minutes.

I got up early to see if she returned. I glanced into the thick forest, praying she was there. I wanted to run towards her, scoop her into my arms, and take her away. I fantasized about kissing her forehead and promising a life where she'd be safe. A home where she wouldn't be threatened. A man who wouldn't treat her as a burden.

I would show her love and become the man to send her home…

But I have no idea how to do that.

Time passed and the forest remained dark.

I am no closer to solving the mystery, so I'll prepare for the morning, waiting patiently for the night.

10:02 AM

After breakfast, we went on our merry way up Mount Donwanago.

Well, as merry as we could be. Pierce sneezed and coughed with every step. Huerta complained we didn't give him enough coffee. Glover glared at me every chance he got.

So, not very merry at all.

I marched with tight lips, answering whatever questions the boys gave me with short responses.

Anderson glanced over his shoulder. His nose scrunched. As we hiked, he slowed to walk next to me. "Are you okay, Second?"

His concerned tone surprised me. "I'm fine, man." I shrugged. "Just lost in thought."

Anderson *humphed*. "If you say so. How is it going with your campers? I finally started to get my guys to warm up to me."

"Halfway there." I jerked my head to the side. "Trying to get the ray of sunshine to talk to me."

Anderson not-so-discreetly looked over at Glover. He clicked his tongue. "He seems like a tough nut to crack, but something is definitely going on beneath his shell."

I snickered. "Your metaphor was pretty good."

Anderson shrugged. "I learn from you, man."

"Second!" Huerta shouted. "Sweeney fell behind again."

I looked over my shoulder to see my cub staring into the forest. Feet glued to the mountain. The white camera trembled in his chubby hands. He appeared troubled. Scared.

My heart drummed in my ears. I hopped down the rock-ledge. "Everything okay, dude?"

Wide eyes darted between the trees. "I saw something," he whispered. He peered through the camera's viewfinder. "Something is following us."

"What did you see?" For the first time, I prayed it was a mountainous predator. "Was it an animal?"

Sweeney shook his head. "It was—"

"Yo, Captain Cyclops, can we get movin'?" Glover snarled. "I wanna get back to camp sometime this week."

"Relax, dude," Huerta retorted. "Sweeney is having an out of body experience."

"What the *duck* is that supposed to mean?" Glover snapped. "Just shout in his face and tell him we've got to move."

"If you want to be Captain, get down there." Huerta pressed his hand against Glover's shoulder.

Glover sucked in a breath through gritted teeth. Swinging his arms, he smacked Huerta in the chest. "Don't touch me. *Ever.*"

Huerta gasped. Brows furrowed, he shoved Glover back. "Like that?"

The cub teetered towards the edge. Steam floated from his ears. "I swear to God, Huerta." Glover balled his fist.

"Whoa, whoa, guys!" I yelled, scrambling to the rock they argued upon. "Enough!"

Their voices rose as their bickering continued. Spit flew and colorful language painted the air between them.

"I saw a ghost!" Sweeney shouted.

The world stilled and my heart sank.

Glover and Huerta stared at the cub in disbelief.

"You started all this because you thought you saw a *ghost?*" Glover growled.

Whatever frustration Huerta had harvested evaporated. "Was it her? Did you see the girl from my—I mean Sparks's—story?"

Sweeney glanced back into the forest. "I-I don't know. But it was definitely a girl. I'm sure of it."

"I'm sure it was just your imagination." I nudged him away from the forest. "Maybe my chili last night was too spicy. You're seeing things."

Huerta laughed. "You call that spicy? That's like saying mint is hotter than a ghost pepper." The cub cackled. "I made a pun."

"Can we just go, *please?*" Glover clasped his hands together and shook them. "I will have manners this time. Let's just keep moving for *ducks* sake."

"Yes, we'll keep moving." I grabbed Sweeney's backpack and dragged him away. "C'mon, buddy."

I heard the flash click and the camera gears whir as an image printed.

"I think she's following us," Sweeney whispered.

"There is no one there, Sweeney," I scolded. "Just keep hiking."

But a flicker of light in the woods to my left proved the cub was right.

1:57 PM

Sunlight beat down on Pack Cottontail as we traversed up the mountainside. Another afternoon of climbing rocks, rocks, and more rocks. Not much fun to document.

But in the midst of the mundane, I saw things. Were they actually sparks flickering between the trees or was it my own imagination? Maybe I really am so white that the mild spices of my trail chili is messing with my brain.

The inclines were not as steep as yesterday but still a tough cardio workout. At first we tried to take the long way around to avoid some scrambling, but it was too long. We were much more cautious. Anderson and a few older cubs scrambled up, ropes ready. The rest ascended slowly and got assistance as needed.

As we walked, I felt eyes staring a hole into the back of my head. Glancing over my shoulder, I caught Glover watching me. Something hid behind his gaze. It was judgmental. Frustrated. Secretive.

My heart pounded. Was he the one who saw me leave last night? Would he say something about my absence?

With the way Glover feels about me, I wouldn't put it past him. Not that I should be worried. I'm his captain. I'm running a tight-ish ship, but mutiny is always possible.

I hung out at the back of the line to try and talk to him. Perhaps he was still frustrated after his fight with Huerta. I needed to understand him better. I hoped to get on his good side by the end of the session.

Not only that, but I don't want him to find out the ghost Sweeney probably saw was *real*. I don't want him to find out that's who I go out and see at night. He needs to know I'm present for my cubs. He needs to think I'm a mentally stable camp counselor that can give him guidance for him to take back home. I only have a few days left at the camp before I'm forced to return to the real world. I only have until then to send her home, too.

Glover gripped the straps of his backpack and kept his eyes forward. He didn't look at me as I hiked next to him.

"How are you doing, man?" I asked.

Silence.

"Have you been enjoying your session so far?"

Glover *humphed.*

My eye twitched. I tried another question: "Have you hiked for this long before?"

No response.

I let out a sigh. "Well, will you tell me why you won't answer me?"

"Your questions are stupid," he spat. "You don't want to get to know me." He picked up the pace to race ahead of me.

That was not the response I expected. The familiarity shocked me. I felt it personally. I didn't like it.

"Glover, hold on." I jogged through the line in an attempt to catch up.

"Second," Atkins called. "Did Sweeney actually see Sparks's ghost this morning?"

I slowed my pace. "Hard to tell." I didn't want to lie. I didn't want Sweeney to feel like he was crazy. Honestly, he wasn't. He probably saw her. I made a vow to myself that I wouldn't push aside another person's claims or emotions. I wouldn't discredit their validity.

I mean, look at me. I have one eye because someone called me a liar. Someone claimed my opinion was invalid.

I won't do that to anyone else. If the boy saw a ghost, then he saw a ghost.

Huerta skidded to a halt. "Wait a second, Second. Does that mean she chose Sweeney as her lover?"

Sweeney choked on his water. He coughed violently as Atkins smacked his back.

"In Sparks's story, he claimed a *man* would save her," Cline corrected. "Sweeney is a minor. It could not be him according to the tale."

A lightbulb brightened above my head. Maybe I didn't have to lie to the boys. Their childlike conviction that this story was fact could work in my favor. They wanted to know the end of the story as I did. What would happen if they perceived me playing along... even though I was living it?

"Cline is right." I puffed out my chest. "Only a man is worthy of her love." I ran ahead and perched upon a rock. "Only a man of strong stature and sound mind can save her from her wooded prison."

Huerta froze. Jaw agape, he grabbed his head and exclaimed, "It makes perfect sense!"

Anderson crossed his arms and chuckled. "I'm not following."

"You don't have to right now." Huerta waved his statement away. "These are only theories."

Glover scoffed and readjusted his backpack. He grumbled and murmured as he kicked up rocks and dust.

"No, no, Glover, I think Captain Second might be onto something," Huerta replied. "We'll have to see with time. But everyone, keep your eyes peeled!"

I shrugged and remained quiet, leaving the rest to their imaginations.

I hope this works.

4:46 PM

Corny jokes and embarrassing high school stories guided the afternoon of our hike. My cubs' personalities shone through their tales. After five days, their shells cracked and we welcomed each other in.

Well, except for Glover. No poop joke or funny comment could melt his icy glare. He hated me, and I wasn't sure why.

The ending point for the day approached *almost* without incident. Almost.

"Captain Second!" a voice shouted. It echoed off the trees.

I skidded to a halt and whipped around to see Huerta pointing into the valley below.

I rushed over and gazed down the cliff side. Thick green trees swayed in the wind. Their leaves blanketed the earth. "What's up, Huerta?"

Sweat beaded on his tan forehead. "I-I saw it."

My heart pounded. Was it GG? Did he see her? "What was it?"

"Was it the ghost?" Atkins gasped.

He pinched his eyes shut. "N-no. Not her. I could have sworn I saw a wolf."

My beating heart didn't calm down. "Are you sure it wasn't a mountain lion?"

"Nah, man, pretty sure it was a big wolf." Huerta spread his arms. "I got a quick look before it disappeared."

It probably was some harmless critter, but I wasn't going to take that chance. "If it's gone, we should move forward." I nudged him back towards the Pack.

"No, dude, that's the problem." He picked up the pace. "I think it's following us."

"What happened?" Anderson called.

A rustling in the bushes stopped the answer from escaping my mouth. All the boys froze and turned to face the bush.

Two yellow eyes peered back.

"Oh *ducks*," Huerta breathed. He turned and bolted.

The worst mistake he could've made.

Sheer panic crept over the remaining cubs. One by one, they chased after Huerta.

My breath caught in my throat. First rule of the wilderness is that you never *run* from a wolf. You can't outrun it.

My cubs became delicious moving targets.

I waited a moment and the rustling stopped. Watching the bushes, my heart leaped. Yellow embers flickered to life, dancing around the bushes.

Huerta saw Ghost Girl's lights.

I turned back and every cub was gone. Anderson shouted over his shoulder, "Second, they're booking it!"

My stomach knotted. She was there. She was calling to me. My feet desired to run toward her. To wrap myself in her presence.

But I couldn't leave my campers alone. "I'm so so sorry, I have to talk to you later," I yelled into the woods. I had no idea if she heard me. I prayed she'd understand.

With no choice, I ran away from GG.

I raced across the rocky terrain, desperate to catch up. My heart pounded in my ears as I clambered up the mountain and wove around trees. My backpack clapped against my back. The pen and pencil Pierce gifted me repeatedly stabbed my spine, but I had no time to fix it.

I shouted ahead, praying they would slow down.

After what felt like forever, I saw them. The earth leveled, dipping down towards the cliffside.

Anderson skidded to a halt at the top of the mountain. His arms flailed to maintain his balance. He shouted for everyone to slow down. His cubs dug their heels into the rock and slowed their pace.

But Sweeney's and Atkins' eyes watched me catch up… but didn't see the line of boys halted in front of them. They sucked in quick breaths as they crashed into the backs of Glover and Madden.

The four of them toppled forward over the edge.

I bellowed Anderson's name and raced to the cliff. Eight arms jutted out and snatched the boys' backpacks. I grabbed Glover's pack and held on. The veins in my arms bulged and my heels dug deeper into the rocks. Screaming bounced around the canyon walls. My muscles burned and my knuckles turned white.

Four arms grabbed my torso and yanked me backward. We landed with a thud. My body crushed two boys but shock froze me. Fire shot down my arms as I lay there staring at the blue sky.

Glover collapsed on top of me. His pulse beat frantically beneath my grip. His chest heaved and his body shook. "No, no, no," he whispered over and over.

A muffled voice vibrated my shoulder. I shifted my weight to lift Glover up and stop crushing the windpipes of Huerta and Pierce.

Huerta rubbed his jaw. "I cannot believe that just happened." His breath hitched with each word.

Madden jumped to his feet and shook out his limbs. "How *ducking* stupid can you be to not notice a *cliff?*" He paced back and forth, rubbing his arms. Tremors shot down his long body.

"It's nobody's fault," I stated firmly.

"Take a look at the meathead who shoved me off the edge and then say that again." Madden sneered, smacking Atkins on the back of the head.

Atkins took the blow but glared at the cub. "You're not the only one who almost avalanched off mountain."

Sweeney wrapped his arms around his backpack and took a deep breath. "We're okay, we're okay, we're okay," he muttered.

"You guys are alive, deep breaths." I gently slid myself away from Glover who still sat close beside me. The boy still hadn't moved. "Are you okay, dude?"

Glover's eyes seemed vacant as if his soul tumbled down the cliffside. His mouth hung open. Goosebumps trailed along his arms.

His shock shot a volt through my soul. Memories pricked my mind.

Sirens.

Shouts.

Swears.

Blood.

My hand flew to the side of my face. I dug my fingertips into my forehead. Damp leather brushed beneath my fingertips. No blood.

I pinched my eye shut and shook my head hard. This wasn't about me. This wasn't me. It was my cub. A boy who needed my help.

Recovering my senses, I asked, "Glover, can you hear me? Are you okay?" The other boys replied right away. I feared his shock paralyzed him.

A moment passed before his gaze lifted to meet mine. "Y-yeah, I think so."

My lips flapped with my exhale. "Thank God." My knees buckled as I staggered to my feet. The other boys helped Glover up.

"I think that's enough hiking for one day," Anderson announced. "Let's make camp nearby."

Anderson led with the cubs close behind.

I traversed slowly across the rocky terrain. My senses heightened after the scare. I felt every pebble beneath my boots. I heard every bug flutter past my head. The world spun and I felt the memories crawling back to the front of my mind.

But Glover's presence beside me pushed the past away. He didn't speak, but he didn't rush up ahead. He didn't glower nor sneer.

We walked together in silence.

Which is the best improvement we could've made.

7:05 PM

I. Am. Exhausted.

Mentally. Physically. Almost emotionally.

When we arrived at the campsite, we threw our packs onto the ground. No one settled down right away. Every cub stood in place, lost in thought.

Some of our campers almost died. Again.

Never in my four years at Camp Southpaw have I endured such hardships. While I've had an unfortunate share of near-death experiences, I never would've thought it'd occur at camp. I mean, yeah, it's a wilderness camp, but this feels different. Feels *intentional.*

Kinda like that movie where those six kids were supposed to be in a plane crash but escaped. So Death chased them one by one.

Oh, God, I'm praying this isn't the case.

I shook my head, bringing myself back. I clapped my hands. "Let's settle in, shall we?"

Everyone nodded and went about their duties.

I started a fire and began cooking dinner. My stomach growled as the oil sizzled and popped. The aroma of chicken floated along the wind. Huerta panicked and claimed the wolf would smell it and come after us. It took a bit of convincing to reassure him that we were safe.

The boys set up their tents then joined us around the campfire. Glover sat across from me. His dark eyes watched me carefully, but he never spoke. Out of the four that almost tumbled off the cliff, Glover appeared the most affected. I checked in on Atkins and Sweeney. They were okay—in better shape than I expected. I tried to talk with Glover, but he remained quiet. I didn't probe.

As our eyes met over the campfire, I knew something was wrong. I knew he needed to tell me something, but I didn't get to ask.

Anderson lathered the chicken in red sauce and cheese, making an excellent trail Chicken Parmigiana. "I think we need to give many prayers of thanks," he stated, handing out the portions.

Cline replaced the piece of chicken he was about to sink his teeth into. "Well, I think it's quite apparent what we all will say."

"We thank God for chicken *breasts*?" Huerta emphasized the last word and smacked his palms against his chest.

Pierce punched his arm. "Not the time, dude."

"I cannot believe it all happened," Atkins mumbled. "I'm definitely thankful for you guys." His gaze fell upon Glover and Madden. "I am so sorry."

Glover's lips sealed, and his eyes locked on the ground.

Madden took a shaky breath. "It's okay, it wasn't your fault." He poked at his food. "We were so worried about one danger we didn't notice the other."

"That's a great lesson for tonight," I said. Taking my journal in hand, I thumbed through the pages. I notated his line in the back of my book. The commentary flowed like a river and I spewed my words of wisdom: "Don't rush into things blind. Panic consumes us, threatening to control our hearts, minds, and bodies. No matter the struggle, no matter the pain, take your time in every situation. Your mind is your own, not your fear's. Take charge, keep both eyes open. Well," I stroked my eyepatch, "for me one."

The cubs chuckled, but Glover's glare burned the edges of my journal. His face grew darker and darker as the boys discussed my spiel, and Anderson's cubs shared their stories for Campfire Chats. The words floated around his head, desperate to penetrate him.

It was too familiar. It was a face reflected in the mirror when I had two eyes.

"That's enough sap for tonight," Huerta announced. He jumped to his feet, the log he perched upon tipped over. "Time to continue my tale."

Tonight, no one objected. Eager eyes watched Huerta as he paced around the firepit.

"Last night, the girl claimed she'd had enough. Her voice cried to the heavens, screaming, 'No more!'" He stood on his tip toes, arms flailing outwards. "No more would he hurt her. No more would she be bruised. The sweet marshmallow was tired of being burned."

"That was a good way to build upon your analogy," I whispered.

Huerta smirked. "He invited her on a date. Not a sweet one with flowers and sunshine. A dark one with death and sorrow. She didn't want to see him anymore." He held up three fingers. "'I hate you,' she yelled." Five fingers. "'Then, you will die here,' he yelled back." Huerta crouched into the dirt. "His threat wasn't empty. She couldn't run. She couldn't hide." He gripped the fallen log with both hands. With a grunt, he raised it above his head. "With so much anger and hatred, he crushed her with all his might." He thrust the log into the fire. Embers crackled and sparks shot from either side.

I swatted them away as they landed on my lap.

Beads of sweat dripped down Huerta's forehead as he walked around the outside of our circle. He raised both hands. "Ten words. Ten words trapped her here. Ten words hurt her forever." He bent forward, sticking his face between Sweeny and Glover. He whispered, "'You'll suffer alone for your afterlife. Forgotten and unloved forever.'"

Glover's breath caught in his throat. His dark eyes brimmed. Huerta's story struck reality. It crept through the cracks of Glover's shell. Whatever he hid slowly seeped out.

My fear is that soon he'll break.

Sweeney stared into the woods. Round eyes wide with fear and searching. He sought something. He waited for something. Was he waiting for *her?*

"I think that's enough for tonight, Huerta," Anderson said. "Your storytelling skills improve every night. Just please make tomorrow night a happier conclusion, okay?" He put a hand on Sweeney's back, bringing the cub back to the campsite.

Huerta shrugged. "The ending all depends on if my theory proves true." He winked at me.

I held back a smile.

That evening, the boys went to bed without another word. We needed to unpack the day. A dark depressing ghost story to end the night. Hiking scares two days in a row. It's as if God got bored with our story and said, "Let's spice things up with some danger." Either that or I'm about to go through another traumatic experience.

I just pray it's the former.

9:58 PM

I waited an extra half hour to ensure Glover slept before sneaking off into the forest. My limbs ached, and my head throbbed, but I had to see her. I needed to talk to her. I ignored her cry before; I needed to make it up to her. Huerta's retelling rekindled the conviction I held in my soul.

I only have a few days until camp ends for the summer. Only a few days left to send her home.

My heart leaped when I saw her. She hovered between the trees. Her dress billowed and floated like a jellyfish under the sea. Adrenaline replaced the exhaustion tugging at my limbs. After today, I needed to feel her warmth more than ever.

She drifted back and forth. Her glowing hand covered her face. Wide eyes shook. Anxiety seemed to entangle her heart.

Leaves crunched beneath my boots as I ran up to her. Her warmth tickled my face. I tugged on my shirt to fix my appearance before remembering she couldn't see. "Hey, are you okay?"

Her dress flickered as she jerked to a halt. "I-I don't know, Second." Her voice shook. "I feel very off lately. I don't know what's wrong. I need to talk to you."

I wondered if she started to realize she was a ghost. "Is there anything I can help with?"

She perched herself upon a rock. White fingers tangled in the edges of her hair.

My heart pounded as I lowered myself beside her. "Tell me everything."

Her back straightened. "My workload has gotten pretty heavy over the past week," she said. "We have a major event next month and if I don't perform well, I won't get the promotion I've been begging for for two years."

I cocked my head to the side. It was not the reply I was expecting. GG was after a promotion? Maybe that's what happened before she died. Maybe she is stuck in this endless loop of reliving her past as if it were the present. I'm praying that if I help her, maybe she will be sent on.

"What are they expecting you to do?"

GG plopped down on and continued to talk about her job. Her words enveloped me like a chrysalis. I stilled, waiting for the moment to break free. I failed to remember everything verbatim. My heart thumped in my chest as I learned more and more about Ghost Girl. I'm going to document a shortened version of what I remember.

GG explained she managed a bunch of people and ensured projects remain on schedule. She didn't tell me what company she works for—or used to when she was alive. They respected her, but didn't reward her. Her financial situation gives her anxiety because she can't afford to move out of her parents home. She ranted a bit about a lazy, *brass*-kissing coworker named Kirk.

"Why don't you speak up for yourself?" I asked. I picked up a leaf and started ripping it in half. Her conversation intrigued me, but my hands needed something to do.

"Because I can do his job better," she blurted. "He is unreliable. He barely completes his projects. And I can do his job anyway, so I just end up taking over and making it ten times better."

I scoffed. "Sounds like you're a perfectionist."

Her lips parted, but then she shut them. "I guess you're right." She threw her hands in the air. "And that's another thing: *he* always makes me feel like I have to be."

The leaf slipped between my fingers. "*He* as in your Kirk?"
She shook her head.

I swallowed the lump in my throat. "Then, your boyfriend?"

"Yes, and he is driving me up a wall."

I ran my fingers through my thick hair. I wanted to make sure I gave her the best advice possible, but honestly, I didn't quite understand her situation.

"Okay, wait, so are you a perfectionist because it's who you are or it's who this *boyfriend* wants you to be?" I spat his title like a curse.

She didn't seem to notice. Her eyes looked distant as she thought. "I think who he wants me to be," she said softly. "He is pushing me to get the promotion. At first I thought he was just being supportive, but—" she stopped.

"But?" I didn't like where this was going. I hated the guy before, but I foresaw myself hating him even more.

She put her hand on her face. "Now that I'm thinking about it, he kinda digs into me if I mess up."

My blood simmered. "What things would he say?"

"A few weeks ago, I missed our date for a multitude of reasons and he was rude about it." She waved her hand. "When we finally went out, he was being all passive aggressive at the table. He was saying things like, 'I know you care more about your job than me' and then like, 'You should work harder if you want to eat at fancy places'. And then he'd tell me not to eat so much."

My blood boiled. What kind of *tish*-head says that to his girlfriend? Someone who is impotent, if you ask me. Any man lucky enough to be GG's boyfriend should shower her with roses whenever she has the *slightest* bad day.

If I was in his shoes? The moment she woke up, I'd prepare coffee and shower her with kisses, hugs, and so much affection that she wouldn't be able to breathe.

I cleared my throat. My heart beat loud in my ears. I forced my mind back to the present. "That's stupid and contradictory."

"Right?" she exclaimed, jumping up. "He's constantly making me feel guilty."

That was a phrase I knew all too well. My last relationship—my whole life—was built up on guilt. I was told "the only one who makes you feel guilty is you". Well, yes, it's in my head, but the circumstances overflowing with passive aggression and slights did not aid my mental health.

GG paced back and forth. "He tends to make me sound stupid in front of my family which frankly, should be impossible."

Also, familiar.

"I can be a bit klutzy sometimes and he loves to tell everyone the embarrassing mistakes I make," she added. "Serious mistakes and not."

My eyes widened. I felt that one, too.

"Also, he—" She stopped pacing. Neck craned, her sightless eyes gazed at the stars. They twinkled and sparkled, but her face darkened. "I'm sorry, I should stop."

"No, no, what else?" My heart raced as I got to my feet. I needed to know everything. What else did he do to her? How much more did I relate? I worried for her. Everything she is feeling, I felt. Fear fluttered around my heart. My story ended with me losing an eye. If she had a life reflective of mine… What did she lose?

A shaky exhale left her full lips. "After we're together, I end up—" She paused. "He makes me cry more than he makes me smile."

My boiling blood bubbled over. She did not deserve that. She deserved a happy ending. She deserved a man to take care of her. Hold her. She should feel safe in his arms. She should want to crash into his open embrace every time she sees him.

That man should *never* make her cry.

GG—this ghost wandering in the woods—didn't get her happily ever after. Do I think they exist? Not for me, of course. Not many get them, I think. But Ghost Girl? She deserved the happiest ending even if it is in the next life.

I balled my fists and sucked in a deep breath. Courage swept into my lungs as I approached her. Emotions swirled in my mind. Frustration, anger, sadness, pity. I knew exactly how she felt. She didn't deserve that.

No one did.

Her pine and lavender scent hooked me, reeling me closer. I wanted to reach out and touch her. I wanted her to know someone cared. Someone was there to listen. Better yet, someone who would listen and keep a secret. Every person I ever vented to told the wrong person. Layers of guilt, "get over it", and "she'll change" piled on top of my mind.

I won't let that happen to her. I will fix her heart and send her home.

"Are you there, Second?" Her voice shook. "I never told another guy about this before. I was told guys didn't care about this kind of stuff."

"Everyone says that," I retorted. My bitterness wasn't for her. It was for everyone else. "Whoever told you must forget that if guys didn't actually care, they wouldn't be in relationships."

Her face froze as my words processed in her brain. "I-I guess that makes sense."

"It takes two to tango, sister. Also, this guy sounds like a total *brass*." I spat the safe-swear without even thinking.

It must have caught her off guard, because she giggled. The frustration around my mind melted away like an ice pop in the sun. Her adorable laugh.

"Second, you never cease to surprise me." A bright smile spread across her face. "Thank you for understanding."

I shrugged. "I didn't do anything but listen."

"You'd be surprised how many people fail such an easy task." She started to raise her hands to clap but lowered them again. "So what would be your advice?"

"Dump him." The words flew out of my mouth before I could grab them. Two syllables fluttered through my fingertips, unable to get back. Red rushed to my cheeks. I didn't know why I was so nervous to say it. I spoke my piece. That is what I wanted to say all along, wasn't it? If she willingly leaves him before things turn for the worst, perhaps she'll be saved and can move on from this life. It's advice I wish I had. If someone told me to dump my ex, I'd still have both eyes.

Those two words hit her hard. She blinked three times. "I can't," she said softly.

My heart pounded. She had to dump him. He was toxic. He was dangerous. He hurt her. "Why not? If you dump him, you won't feel the need to be a perfectionist. Then, you can focus on enjoying your job rather than stressing."

Anti-gravity hair floated around her face. He soft lips parted, but she said nothing.

I stepped forward. My limbs shook as I lifted my hand. I brought my fingers closer. Closer. They hovered by her locks. I wanted to push the hairs behind her ear. My lips tingled. I wanted to press my lips to hers and melt away her sadness. I only wanted her to be happy.

My stomach twisted, and I pulled my hand back. My fingers tremored. I've never been so nervous. Perhaps it's because I've never touched a ghost before. Perhaps it's because I've never felt such raw emotion towards another person.

A soul I genuinely care about.

"You're right," she whispered, placing her hands side by side. "Just because I understand him doesn't mean he understands me."

He doesn't understand her, and yet she's still with him? What self-righteous *brass*-hole doesn't care enough to know every small detail about their girlfriend? If it were me, I'd take the time to learn the littlest things. Everything from her biggest fears to her coffee order. I wanted to say more, but she cut me off.

"Thank you, Second." Her eyes widened. "You're definitely a writer because your words are wise."

I shook my head. "It's just unfortunate experience."

She frowned. "Well, if you've experienced what I have, then my heart breaks for you. Next time, it's your turn to talk." She closed her hands and disappeared.

My heart breaks for you.

Five words tapped at the glass surrounding my soul. Each one left a crack that spread across my body.

She didn't know anything about my past. All she knows is I have one eye from a bad falling out.

And yet, she still hurts for a man she's never met. A story she's never heard.

My soul is both comforted and sorrowful.

August 8

DAY 4 OF THE HIKING TRIP

10:07 AM

"Just because I understand him doesn't mean he understands me."

GG's words played over and over in my head the next morning. My blood boiled at the thought of her relationship. I wished I could cross the planes of existence to sock her boyfriend right in the face.

"Captain Second, how much further?" a whiny voice penetrated my thoughts.

I returned to the present and locked my mind to remain there. I needed to be lively for these boys. Two near death experiences was two too many.

I looked over my shoulder. Huerta's feet dragged against the rocks as he grumbled and complained about his ankles.

I tightened my backpack straps. "We're on day four and there are six days of the trip."

Huerta blew a raspberry. "Nooo. I meant until we get to the good views."

"I… agree…" Cline panted. Breath fogged his round glasses. "We've… been… surrounded…"

"By trees and rocks and trees," Atkins finished for him.

I couldn't argue with the boys. Hiking with no ending in sight made every step heavier. The views were the best part.

"Aren't rocks and trees what nature is all about?" Anderson butted in. "But we should be seeing the best view today." He pulled his map taut.

I looked over his shoulder. Our path increased difficulty from that point on. The best news? We'd hit the highest peak by the end of day. After that, we'd be on our way back down.

I prayed for no more near-death experiences. All the boys needed to return to Camp Southpaw in one piece.

As we continued our journey, I thought of the previous days. First we ran away from angry captains after a prank. Then, we ran for our lives. The boys were in surprisingly good spirits after everything that transpired.

Although, I didn't feel Glover's eyes on me as much.

I looked back to see the camper with his head hung low. Dark eyes stuck to the boots that stomped across the earth.

"*You don't want to get to know me.*" Glover's words replayed in my head. Something moved beneath the surface. I know I'm not a therapist. I know I'm not his parent. But I am his captain for the session, which meant he was my responsibility.

I swapped places with Anderson and retreated to the back of the line. My co-captain understood the assignment and kept the pack moving forward while playing a guessing game to pass the time.

I hiked beside Glover. He didn't acknowledge my presence at first. He focused on the rocks he crushed with his feet as our elevation changed. Stones rolled behind him as he marched up the mountain. He seemed on a higher alert after the incident.

We started to scramble up the next stretch when I cleared my throat. "Glover, how are you doing after yesterday?"

He remained quiet. His fingers wrapped around the rock above him. Baggy sleeves fell around his elbows.

A lump caught in my throat when I finally noticed.

Scars painted stripes on Glover's forearm.

My heart twisted in my chest, and my footing slipped. No wonder Glover was bitter. No wonder he didn't want to be touched. No wonder he hated me. I regretted every negative comment I thought towards him. Here was a boy crying for help. Someone needed to answer it.

I pulled myself up another two feet. "Glover, you told me yesterday that you said I didn't want to get to know you."

His body jerked to the left. Stones tumbled down the mountainside beneath his feet.

I jutted a hand out and clasped his back. I pressed his thick backpack against him, keeping him close to the mountain.

He locked eyes with me. Sadness, anger, bitterness swirled in his dark irises. He was frustrated. Stressed.

When you're lost in the woods with only your thoughts, everything surfaces.

"It's because you *don't* want to know me," he snarled, squirming away from my touch. He picked up the pace.

My biceps burned, but I quickened uphill. "Or is it because you won't let me?"

"It doesn't matter," he snapped.

"Glover," I called. "Yes, it does."

He stopped climbing and looked down at me. Water lined his eyelids. Any more and they would overflow. "If you really wanted to know me, wouldn't you remember my first name?"

I froze. We never called the kids by their first names. We rarely even looked at them on their sheets. Only if kids' last names matched would we resort to first names. All our cubs were so unique, I didn't even look.

"That's what I thought." He scoffed. He turned away and climbed faster.

Calves on fire, my palms gripped the rocks and I pulled myself up to stay alongside him. I needed to prove that I wanted to know him. To prove I wanted to help him. "Can we start by me asking you your name?"

"No, you have to earn that."

First time I ever had to earn someone's name.

Wait, second time. Ghost Girl was first.

I wonder how she would respond to this situation? She seemed to have good insight. She had her own struggles—as does everyone—but she seems like the kind of girl to be motherly. Caring and kind. The one to bottle up her struggles so as not to seem weak to those she's taking care of.

Was that the same with Glover?

"Fine, challenge accepted, Glover. I will earn your name."

The cub's surprised face and small smile warmed my heart.

Finally, we reached the top. I swung my leg over the ledge until I was firmly kneeling on the ground. I reached down for Glover's hand.

He looked at it for a moment like it would hurt him. His expression softened after a moment. Then, he took it. I yanked him up.

He had accepted my help.

A good start to a tough journey.

2:03 PM

I prayed I made it up. I prayed it was simply paranoia festering in my head. But I know they spotted her. She was bright. She was shiny. She was beautiful. How could they not have noticed?

Relax, Second. Maybe only one or two saw her. Perhaps I could persuade them to keep quiet or play along with Huerta's fantasies. Think back to who it might have been.

The other cubs beckoned Glover to rejoin them, so I didn't get to ask him anything too personal after our chat. It was fine; Huerta claimed him as his "baby bear"—as he called it. While I stayed in the rear, Anderson reinforced the buddy system in case of an emergency. It sucked it was an actual concern now.

As we continued our way through the woods, I heard her. A cry for me: "*Second, I don't know if I can do this.*" Ghost Girl's whisper was louder than the chirping cicadas. Red rushed to my face and I looked around to see if anyone noticed.

They carried on their conversations as if nothing happened.

The butterflies returned to my stomach, but anxiety partied with them. GG needed me. She needed my help. I promised I would do what I could to send her home, but I couldn't do it at that moment.

I panicked. How could I sneak away to tell her I'd meet up with her later? I could say I needed to take a *tish*, but I still didn't know about the time jumps. A few moments with her could be an hour in the real world.

"Captain Second!" Huerta called. "You gotta come see this!"

His shout snapped me back into reality. I ran up the hill to catch up. My heart pounded. Did they see her? What would they do?

"What's up?" I replied as calmly as possible, cresting the hill.

Huerta and the other boys stood at the edge. A smile spread across his face. "We finally have a view." He extended his arms like a king overlooking his kingdom.

I let out a shaky breath. A view. Good. We needed a view. I met up with the boys on the edge and gazed upon the valley.

Broccoli like trees stood tall across the three mountains. Blue sky met the green and everything blended into a perfect picture. Crisp air filled my lungs as I drank in the scene. It was pure. Peaceful. To our right awaited the final incline for Mount Donwanago: the last scramble that made calves scream and biceps burn. A feat not for the faint of heart.

But my heart wasn't in it. It jumped out of my chest, running back to her as she cried for me again: *"Second, he is with my family right now. I can't do this."*

The pulse in my head throbbed. I needed to find her. I needed to say something encouraging to her, no matter how brief.

"Hey, Captain Second," Pierce said beside me.

I jumped out of my skin. How long had he been standing there? Hand on my chest, I exhaled, "Pierce, don't do that."

"Sorry, I thought you heard me before." Pierce lifted a hand. "We're stopping for lunch before we head up."

I glanced over my shoulder. The boys perched themselves upon rocks and stumps. Three dangled their legs over the cliff side.

Sweeney took out his instant-print camera. His thick hands wrapped around it like a child holding a drink cup. He snapped a picture of the cubs. The photo slid out of the top; black and undeveloped. He placed it in his large stack.

Everyone was distracted. The perfect time to sneak away. Even if I was there for two minutes and it ended up being fifteen minutes our time, they would be packing up.

"Thanks, Pierce." I patted his back. "I've gotta do some business and then journal a bit."

He laughed. "Okay, I'll tell Anderson." He joined the others.

I had a moment—but only a moment. I looked down at my watch. Its scratched face blurred the numbers. A little after two.

I took a deep breath and ran into the woods to find her.

The brush scraped my arms as I raced deeper into the forest. I needed to be quick to find her. Otherwise our time together would shorten.

A disheartened voice cut through leaves. *"Second, please."*

I tasted lavender and pine as I inhaled. Almost there. The warmth grew hotter like the burning sun. Golden rays cut through the brown trunks.

I burst into her clearing. I sucked in gulps of air. "I'm here."

Her figure froze and spun around to face me. "Second, they're calling me downstairs. What do I do?"

"Is it about dumping your boyfriend?"

She nodded frantically. "Yes, I'm trying, I promise, but he isn't letting me." She hovered across the clearing, heading into the forest.

I reached for her, but she floated away from me. I caught up and followed her through the woods. "Why won't he? Just lay down the law. He's toxic."

"I know, I know, that's what my friend says." Her pace quickened as her figure wove through the trunks. Anxiety radiated from her translucent curvy body. "But he is trying to manipulate my family now."

"Won't they listen to you?"

"It's not that easy!" She exhaled sharply. "They have connections with him and they'd probably hate me if I broke them." She floated faster toward the edge of the forest. In the direction of my campers.

Panic stung my soul. What would happen if the guys saw her? Would she ever show up again? Would she be lost in the woods before I could even save her?

I needed to stop her. I needed to make her think and go back to her realm and dump her Ghost Boyfriend. "What makes you happy?"

Her body jerked to a stop. The edge of the woods was in sight. I wanted her to head back to her clearing, but I didn't think I could grab a ghost and shove her aside. Besides, I didn't want to startle her.

"What makes me happy?" She wondered aloud. "I love my family. I love the way the wind feels in my hair or the sound my arrows make when they hit their mark." Glowing fingers tapped her face. "I do love my job and my work—except Kirk, of course. Coffee is something I look forward to." Glossy eyes found me. Despite lacking sight, they searched my soul. They found my pounding heart and lingered there. "I look forward to your words."

I sucked in a breath. She—she—what? She looked forward to my words? To me? Why? She knows the bare minimum about me.

Perhaps it's because I'm the first person who can see her in these woods.

"I appreciate that." Gratitude and sincerity wove between my words, and they touched her face.

A smile spread across her cheeks. "Of course. I wish you could be here to do this for me."

I nodded. "It would be easier if someone else could solve it, but you have to stand up for yourself. Out of all the things that make you happy: your boyfriend wasn't among that list."

GG bit her lip. Sadness floated around her like a rain cloud. I wanted to rush up and shove it away. To hold an umbrella above her head and keep the sorrow from pouring down. But there was only so much I could do to help her. She needed to finish this herself before she could move on.

I took a few steps forward. The noises of the forest faded as I stood before her. The shouts of the boys in the distance warbled like they were underwater. Sunlight radiated from her body and enveloped me like a blanket. It was vibrant. Glowing. I was a sunflower and kept turning to her.

"So, what are you going to do now?" I asked.

Her head faced mine. Her chin tilted up. I felt her looking at me, even if she could not see.

My stomach was a frat house for butterflies. They partied hard as I stood next to her. She seemed small and delicate. I wanted to wrap my arms around her and protect her.

But she had to stick up for herself first.

"I-I am going to tell my family the truth." Her voice wavered, but she forced confidence in it. "I will do what it takes to make me happy."

"Make you happy and *peaceful*," I added. "Some happiness is fleeting. Most of it robs peace. But I'm confident getting rid of this guy is what you need to move on." I tried to grab the last two words back. I didn't want her to go.

"Yes. Move on." She placed her palms side by side. "My heart needs to move on to give myself peace."

Was this it? If she completed this task would I ever see her again? I leaned forward. My lips lingered an inch from her forehead. I wanted to feel her. At least once before she left. Before she moved on. I wanted her to know there was a guy that *never* considered her a bother. Who never thought her stupid or incompetent.

But I couldn't do it.

I stood upright and cleared my throat. "Will you come back to tell me what happened?"

She smiled. "Of course. But please, be here. I know time is weird, but I have a feeling I'll need you more than ever."

My breath hitched; my body ached. I drank in every syllable. Every possible meaning behind her sentence. I never realized words of affirmation was one of my love languages. I craved being needed and desired more than gifts or touch or acts.

"I promise I will be here for you." My fingers extended to brush her hair but each strand wiggled away from me. "Keep calling for me, I'll answer."

A soft smile, a quiet clap, and she was gone.

The noises of the woods banged against my ears. The rushing stream, the chirping cicadas, and the camera shutter snaps.

My heart froze. Tremors shot through my legs as I forced my body to look up.

A shadow of two boys darted to the right.

3:45 PM

On the outside, I was cool and collected. Nothing ever happened. I went to journal in the woods, use nature's facilities, and was on my way back. It took a half-an-hour, sure, but I couldn't be rushed, right? They all bought it right? They didn't know I spent twenty minutes with her and ten to write my last entry. My face shows I'm well rested and ready for the last stretch of Mount Donwanago. By nightfall we'd arrive at the highest peak.

Internally, I panicked.

I stamped this entry at 3:45 rather than the time I sat to document. It was the start of our final ascent. The start of the countdown before GG is discovered.

My legs screamed as we climbed the steep mountain. It was worse than the one Pierce slid down. How some of these hikes are legal for a children's camp amazed me. Normally, I'd welcome the challenge. Face it head on. But I think the stress of keeping GG secret got to my head.

I held up the rear, keeping my eye peeled. I watched each boy's movements. Their gazes. I waited for something to give away the two that saw me with GG.

We sang the camp song twelve times before I noticed the suspicious looks.

Glover's side-eyes were more frequent than usual. However, this time confusion reflected in the glint of his dark irises. Not hatred. Not judgment.

My stomach twisted. I accepted his challenge to earn his name. After saving his life yesterday, I hoped he'd be more open. But if he saw me talking to a ghost in the woods? Maybe whatever head-way I made became null and void. He might think I'm crazy and unstable, drowning myself in a "ghost story" instead of facing responsibility.

But I wouldn't let him down.

The trail leveled to a steep incline rather than a scramble. I snatched a tall stick off the wooded path. Using it for support, I hiked faster to catch up with Glover who tried to quicken his pace. I wouldn't let him.

"How are you holding up, Glover?"

He kept his eyes straight ahead. Lips tight.

I jabbed my stick between two rocks. They tumbled behind us in a mini avalanche as we continued our ascent. I needed one sentence. One topic. Something to bond over to break through Glover's barrier, letting the stones fall. He didn't need to tell me his life story. He didn't even need to tell me his favorite color.

I needed him to accept that I genuinely wanted to know more about him.

We walked in silence. The boys' voices grew louder around me, but I didn't jump into any conversations like usual. Time was running out.

Glover's eyes glued to the ground and his shoulders raised to his ears.

I wouldn't beat around the bush anymore. Glover was secretive and vague. Someone needed to give it to him straight. I asked bluntly: "Do you think the world hates you?"

His boot caught on a stone. His body jerked forward and he sucked in a sharp breath.

I grabbed his shoulder and snatched his pack, yanking him backwards.

His eyes widened. He stopped for a moment and stared at me. He shook his head hard. "Stop doing that," he grumbled, trying to tear himself away. "And I'm not going to answer."

I clutched the backpack harder. "Well, the world doesn't hate you, and I'm not going to let you get hurt, Glover. I thought yesterday was proof enough."

"You're just doing your job." His steps grew louder. "You get paid to care."

I laughed. He has no idea how low my bank account is. "My dollar-an-hour counselor job? If I wanted to make money caring for people, I would've gone into medicine."

Glover smirked. "Do you really only make a dollar each hour?"

I smiled. I was finally getting to him. "Sure do. Every summer I've come here to hide in the woods and help boys grow in life."

He scoffed. "Life? Sounds to me like you don't have one."

Glover got me there. But I wouldn't say I have *no* life. More like, the life I had I've been trying to restart. He doesn't need to know the details. "Well, I wouldn't say *that*. I'm still trying to figure that part out."

"I think you're getting kinda old." Glover hopped up on a rock and looked down at me. "Clock's ticking, Grandpa Second."

"I'm going as fast as I can." I glanced down at my watch. "But unfortunately, I can't do anything until we're out of these woods." I jumped upon his boulder. "So why don't we pick up the pace so I can go find my life?"

Glover mocked a salute. "Aye, aye, Captain."

I couldn't hide my smile. Progress.

Huerta rejoined his Baby Bear. "Glover, my son." He flung his arms around the boy and wailed, "Why did you leave me?"

Glover's voice muffled in Huerta's sleeve. "You sound like a dying cat."

Huerta gasped. "Are you saying my acting is bad?"

"Terrible." I butted in. "You might not want it as your college major."

Huerta stuck his chin up. "For your information, I wasn't even planning on it, because I don't need it." He turned around and dramatically shoved aside Atkins and Cline.

"You're trying too hard, Huerta!" I shouted.

"I am going to ignore you, good sir," Huerta retorted and continued walking.

Cline shrugged his shoulders. "So much for the buddy system. He's supposed to stay with Glover."

"Glover is tough, he can handle himself." Atkins winked at his fellow camper.

Glover scoffed. "Yeah, because I'd trip you and feed you to the wolves." A joke hid between his threat. Hopefully.

"What can someone actually do to stop a wolf before it eats you?" Cline wondered aloud.

"Don't run, that's for sure." I laughed. "They don't teach you important skills like that in school."

"What did you go to college for, Captain Second?" Cline asked.

"Nothing too exciting." I shared a bit about my experience in college going through the general education and creative writing programs. The best of times, the worst of times. Surprisingly, they were interested in what I had to say. They asked questions, joked, and remained invested in my stories. My cubs were shocked to see a nerd like me as a legendary counselor at a wilderness camp.

"I needed an escape." I helped Sweeney up the hill. "When you get older, things tend to get overwhelming. Always have a healthy outlet when times get tough."

"Don't tell me what to do." Glover smirked.

Cline panted as he grabbed Atkins hand for support. "He… is… right… though."

"It's like when you play video games if people are annoying," Atkins said.

"Or when you eat your feelings away?" Huerta pretended to bite my walking stick.

I yanked it away and laughed. "Better to talk about those feelings than eat them."

Glover rolled his eyes. "We're not little *glitches*, Second. Guys don't talk about their feelings."

I held back a sigh. That *ducking* toxic phrase. The ridiculous notion that guys' mental health doesn't need improvement. We punch it out and are fine. Does that work? Sometimes, yes. But we can't hit girls, and she was my problem.

Anderson interrupted before I could answer. Looking down at us, he waved with a big smile on his face. "We finally made it!"

5:03 PM

The view was worth every ache. Every muscle spasm. The top of Mount Donwanago was a sight to behold.

Thousands of trees like small puffs of green across the valley. The sun set in the west behind the peaks. Streaks of yellow light cut through orange clouds. Mountains stretched hundreds of miles, and the scent of sap tickled my nose. The world seemed so far away. I felt like a great giant and a small ant simultaneously. Everything in the palm of my hand and yet so high above me.

I stood beside my co-captain. Contentment spread across his face. "What a way to end our final year as counselors," Anderson said.

I didn't want to think about it. Facing the real world for an entire year and then every year after that? No excuse to unplug for three months?

A pang of guilt struck me. Ghost Girl didn't get a chance to experience the real world anymore. She was trapped in the woods until she broke up with her toxic boyfriend and became her own person.

But when she passes on, I'll feel alone again. Facing the memories alone. The other captains are my friends, sure, but we rarely get deep. With Ghost Girl, it came naturally. Was it because she was blind to the mistake streaked across my face?

The scars beneath my eyepatch throbbed. The past stung as my remaining iris soaked in the color of the sunset. My blind eye yearned to escape the darkness it hid behind.

My soul couldn't let go of mistakes. I thought another climb would clear my head enough. I thought another night on top of a mountain would vanquish the worry and fear I've felt since the accident.

It didn't. The only time I began to forget was when I was with Ghost Girl.

Why? I was supposed to be helping her. Why was she helping me?

"Captain Second, are we making camp here?" Huerta called. "I'm hungry."

I shook my thoughts away. The boys needed me first. I'd be with Ghost Girl this evening.

But, would she? Did she break it off with her boyfriend? Did she go home?

Part of me prayed she succeeded and she was at peace. The selfish side of me prayed she failed and would run back to me.

I don't know which one I'm hoping for more.

8:09 PM

With bellies full of Fettuccine Alfredo, we sat around the campfire watching the sun disappear behind the mountains.

Two men, twelve boys, fourteen unique stories.

Only two stories left to tell: Glover's and mine.

I started Campfire Chats because I wanted to normalize boys talking about their feelings to other young men that would listen and understand.

Although, I never tell the truth. I never delve into the events of my past that led me to Southpaw. I never say the real reason why I walk the streets voluntarily wearing an eyepatch. I started this trend at camp, but I never followed through.

What does that say about me?

Anderson clapped his hands. "This is the climax of our hike—quite literally. This means all the deep *tish*, all the questions, everything is talked about here. Nothing ever leaves the mountain. No judgment." He dragged his index finger through the air. "If any one of you laughs during something serious, whispers, or talks bad, we will not tolerate it."

Anderson's cub—Madden—waved a hand. "We know the drill, man. Ain't nobody a snitch."

"Or a little *glitch*," Ortiz added.

The boys laughed. The invisible weight lifted from our campsite like fog rolling off the mountainside. I was blessed to have a group that took this seriously. It's been five days since I met them, and they've already matured. Whatever we did worked, and I was grateful.

"Today is our sixth night together. Over the past few days, twelve stories have been shared in some capacity. Which means there are two left." Anderson gestured to Glover and myself.

My camper and I locked eyes. A silent understanding.

Neither of us would share our full stories.

Anderson leaned back on his log. "Who wants to go first?"

Glover made no noise, so I volunteered. I cleared my throat. "Hi, everyone. I'm Captain Second."

"Hi, Second," they replied in unison.

I chuckled. "You guys pretty much heard my story during the last stretch."

Huerta raised an eyebrow. "You know what we *really* want to hear during this Campfire Chat." He pointed to his eye.

It's the story everyone waited for, but one I wouldn't tell honestly.

"I figured." I felt their gazes through the eyepatch. My lips formed the familiar words that I shared for the past four years. A fabricated lie. One I perfected every time I told it. "I lost my eye a few years back in an accident." That much was true. "I was a bit of a party boy in high school." Half-true. "I drank a bit too much one night but didn't want to stay over." Fabrication. "I thought I was fine to drive—I mean, you always do. So, I took the keys from my friend and drove home." Half-truth. "I wasn't paying attention." Lie. "I think you know the rest." False.

Silence lingered. A few shifted uncomfortably. It was apparent some drank underage. I was not there to judge. My fabricated story was supposed to be a lesson. Whether they believed me or not was on them.

It was a simpler message than the truth.

I looked over at Glover who would share his story next. Dark eyes glowed in the firelight. If his irises could speak, they'd spit one word:

Liar.

I waited for the callout. I waited for someone to say, *"You just wear an eyepatch to scare us."* Or, *"Show us your scar so we know you're not lying."*

But it never came. Not from Glover. Not from Huerta. None of them.

It hurt more. Why? Why did their belief hurt me more? Because they trusted me enough to take my story without question.

And I lied to them.

Would Ghost Girl react the same? Did I gain her trust enough that she wouldn't second-guess my story?

Anderson clapped. "Thank you, Captain Second. I know your story isn't easy to tell."

His words sharpened the guilt that cut my heart.

No, it's not easy to tell. That's why I never tell it.

"Glover, are you ready?" Anderson asked.

The cub nodded. "If you couldn't tell, I'm a bit of a loner," he began, knotting his fingers "Don't fit in much, not many friends, blah, blah, you know the cliche."

Huerta chuckled, and Pierce elbowed him.

"It's not that nobody wants to be my friend," Glover continued, "but it's that I keep myself apart. I like my space. Distance is good for watching and waiting." His gaze locked with mine.

I felt his thoughts. He wanted me to know every word coming out of his mouth was a lie. His fabrication would match mine in believability. No one would doubt his story either.

"I keep myself apart because I wait to see what I can do to fit in," Glover said. And that was the end. Period. Paragraph break.

I saw through his story. Every word had a double meaning. A message wove between the lines. Did Glover want me to figure it out or was it a taunt? A game to say, *I know you are keeping secrets. So I'll keep mine.*

I told Glover I'd earn his name. I'll prove to him he doesn't need to retain a distance.

The boys clapped and thanked Glover for sharing. A few shared words of encouragement, insisting they never thought Glover to be a black-sheep.

We're all puzzle pieces. Different shapes, different patterns, different purposes. But we all fit in to make one big picture. The point of life is to find out where we fit.

My problem is I'm twenty-four and still unsure of where I belong. My accident reset my life. I've been hiding in the woods.

But Glover? His life goes on. He can find his place much sooner than me. He just needs a nudge in the right direction.

I hope I can give that to him, somehow.

10:04 PM

I couldn't leave. It would've been worse. I prayed for her to fail, but I wasn't there when she fell. I should have been there. I wasn't.

I pray she will forgive me.

We chatted around the fire until late into the night. S'mores stuck upon our lips as we shared stories of crazy high school teachers and wild homeroom pranks. No one asked Glover nor me any questions.

We were about to go to bed when Huerta added his own flavor to the Ghost Story he finished retelling yesterday.

"His curse trapped her here. She's lurking in the woods." Huerta raised his arms and lurched forward. "Like a zombie, she waits until the boys are asleep. We are now at the highest peak. The highest point in our trip." He wrapped his arms around Sweeney. "We are ripe for the picking. When she comes back—" Huerta squeezed until Sweeney's face turned red, "she'll *kill us!*"

Sweeney tapped Huerta's arm twice, and the cub let go.

"Captain Second, we might need to fact check that one." Cline pointed to my journal. "I don't think she's a hostile ghost."

"I didn't think she was either," Atkins murmured.

"Y-you promised to tell the happy ending tonight!" Sweeney stammered. Goosebumps trailed his arms.

"What's wrong, Sweeney?" Huerta teased. He wiggled his fingers and sang as hauntingly as he could, "Are you afraid of ghoooooosts?"

The boy nodded. Round eyes wide. He opened his mouth to speak, but when his gaze met mine, he shut it as if his words would hurt me.

Glover didn't care. His gaze darted between Sweeney and me. The corners of his mouth turned upward. "He isn't being a little *glitch*. His fear is real because we saw one." He jerked his chin toward me. "Didn't we, Captain Second?"

My face turned whiter than the marshmallows. It froze my insides until my heart stopped beating in my chest.

He saw me. He saw me with her.

Glover's eyes spoke louder than his words. He knew I was a liar. He knew my story around the campfire was fake. I wanted to get close to him, but he didn't trust me. So, he'd break me until the lies crumbled at my feet.

Half of me doesn't blame him. How could I? The relationship that cost me an eye was built upon a rocky foundation of deceit. Constant lies. Constant tricks. Constant doubt.

If I can't open up, how did I expect him to?

Twenty-six eyes stared at me. Their irises gave away their perception of Glover's claims. Some believed I saw a ghost. Others were content with a story. The rest were ready for more.

I ignored the bead of sweat crawling down my temple. "Which ghost are you talking about? Christmas past, present, or future?" I replied.

The boys laughed. My shoulders relaxed, but Glover's spine straightened.

"You know the Ghost I'm talking about," Glover snapped. "The pretty one."

Ooooohs and dozens of questions erupted from the cubs. Was she my "Canadian" girlfriend? Was she possessing me? Was her dress see-through? Was she actually the ghost from the story?

"She might be Canadian, I didn't ask." I stoked the fire. I wished the flames would consume me. I wished to turn back time and stop Glover and Sweeney from seeing me.

"Well, what is this ghost, exactly?" Anderson asked. "Is Sparks actually *not* insane?"

"It's some girl Second meets with secretly." Glover popped a marshmallow into his mouth. His next sentence was muffled, but I wished I didn't understand it: "He also writes love notes to her in his diary."

My heart beat unsynchronized. Wild. Erratic. Any moment it would stop.

No. I would take control of the situation. I needed to play along.

I forced a laugh. "Love notes? I'm no poet, so I hope this girl likes cheesy pickup lines."

My cubs laughed. Red rushed to Glover's cheeks. Not embarrassment. Anger.

"You're crushing on her even though she's dead," Glover snarled.

"You sneak out to see her every night. I bet you're constantly thinking about her."

"Wait, wait, wait," Huerta interjected, arms up. "Glover, so you're telling me my theory is true? Sparks's ghost girl is following us?"

Glover growled, "Yes."

"And Captain Second goes out and talks to her? Like I *said* yesterday?"

Red crawled up Glover's neck. "Yes!"

Huerta leaned back and clapped slowly. "Captain Second, you are a brave soul, facing this apparition all by yourself. You are a noble knight off to save her."

Glover's confused expression mirrored mine.

"I didn't get to finish the finale of my tale!" Huerta leapt to his feet. He wielded his roasting stick like a sword. "Alas, she waits in the woods. Crying. Screaming. Waiting. Waiting. *Waiting!*" His voice wailed. "She craves a love that was stolen from her!"

Cline streaked marshmallow over his red superhero shirt. "In Sparks's story, if the Ghost Girl falls in love with a man, she will be saved."

Huerta growled and threw his stick into the fire. "Cline, this was *my* grand finale! Why you gotta be a little *brass*-hole."

In the heat of Glover's accusations, I had forgotten Huerta alluded to that yesterday. I played along. "You're welcome, everyone. I am sacrificing my sanity to save the Ghost Girl." I bowed. "There is no need to worry if she'll kill you as Huerta suggests."

Glover's knuckles turned white as he clutched his roasting stick. "No, no, it's not the stupid story."

"But it is!" Huerta leaped to his feet. "I mean it's not stupid, but the Ghost Girl haunts these woods because a lover abandoned her. She cries and moans awaiting a new man to save her." He kneeled beside me and thrust out his hands. "Behold, her savior. Captain Second."

My cheeks burned. I wanted to be her savior. I wanted to be the one to whisk her away. When the sun set, I wanted to be the man she thought of. When she desired a hand to hold, I wanted her to think of mine. When loneliness snuck in her room at night, I wanted to be the one she called.

But guilt hid behind every want. I had prayed she failed her task and stayed in this life with me. If she did fail, would she ever forgive me?

Everyone but Glover clapped at Huerta's conclusion. I couldn't tell who seriously believed Sparks's story and who loved to play along.

Glover's eyes glowed red. His roasting stick snapped; its shards scattered around his boots. Bitterness seeped through his teeth.

I swallowed the lump in my throat. The bonds we formed over the past two days melted like metal in lava. I prayed I could reshape it in the morning.

Anderson rose from his perch and cracked his back. "Happy to hear the ghost won't eat us. Now, I think it's time for bed, guys."

Glover's brow furrowed. The corner of his lip turned upward. "The rest of the trip will be easy." His low voice rumbled.

Huerta took the bait. "Yeah, we don't need sleep! We can rest easy with Captain Second here on the campsite. The ghost loves him, so we're safe." He raised a tin mug filled with leftover marshmallows. "Let's stay up later tonight! I'll serenade you all with a selection from my meme-song-repertoire."

"Let's add another challenge on top of that." Glover's eyes shot daggers through me. "Why don't we see who can stay up the latest?"

The blades drew blood. Glover wanted to keep me from her. He wanted to torment me. Even if Anderson and I ordered the boys to go to sleep, this challenge would not go unaccepted. One of the boys would see how long he could stay awake. If she cried for me in the middle of the night, I wouldn't be able to see her.

Anderson waved a hand and plucked his sleeping bag off the floor. "As long as no one passes out or attracts dangerous wildlife."

"Or ghosts!" Huerta interjected.

"Or ghosts—then I don't care." Anderson rolled out his bag and fluffed his small camper pillow. "Just don't be too loud."

The boys chatted and made snack bets on who would stay awake the longest. I didn't want to participate, but they forced my hand. I remained seated around the dwindling fire.

Glover sat across from me. Orange flames set his eyes alight. He knew he won. He knew I couldn't leave. With Huerta's dedication, it would be impossible for me to escape without him following.

I wrote in my journal for a bit, wishing I could redo this evening and somehow fix all of this.

Now, I'm praying to God that Ghost Girl succeeded in her task and finally went home.

11:47 PM

Ghost Girl, I'm sorry.

I'm sorry.

I'm sorry.

I hear you crying. I hear you calling my name.

What happened? Why can't you move on?

I know I promised I would be there for you. And I will be. I want to be.

I am here. I am here. Please, I'm so sorry. I can't leave.

They're still awake. Glover's eyes are peering at me through the dark. Huerta is mumbling to the other boys.

I can't leave. For your sake.

I'm so, so sorry.

August 9

DAY 5 OF THE HIKING TRIP

3:33 AM

Ghost Girl, please. I wish you could hear me. I'm whispering to you. Trying to reply.

I tried to get up. To run to you.

But Glover was still awake. He bolted upright in his sleeping bag. A flash of light cut through the dark.

My breath caught in my throat. I shoved a hand over my eyepatch and staggered back. I hated how the bright light recalled dark memories.

Lights.

Glass.

Sirens.

Screams.

Blood.

The memories flashed by my eyes in the brightness of the flashlight.

I turned away. "Don't do that," I whispered to him.

Click. Darkness. Silence.

I let out a shaky breath and looked over my shoulder. "What are you doing?"

Glover paused. "If you leave, I'll wake all of them up and tell them to follow you."

My chest ached. I should have just gone. I should have just run away, not caring what Glover thought.

But I didn't. I lay back down. Worried about what he would do. Worried about what the others thought of me. Did they think you were real? Would they call me crazy for running after you?

Would they call me a liar?

I journaled for a few minutes to keep myself awake, hoping Glover would fall asleep. Praying exhaustion would get the better of him.

But white eyes still glow in the dark.

Ghost Girl, I'm sorry.

I'm sorry.

I'm sorry.

9:08 AM

Sleepless. Heartbroken. Sorrowful.

My night in three words.

My feet trudged through mud as we packed our things to head back down Mount Donwanago. The bags under my eye deepened as I looked up toward the sun. I wished it would burn me up. Turn me to ash so the wind would blow me away. The more I was haunted, the more I wished to become the haunter. God, make me transparent and lifeless.

Then, I can be with Ghost Girl forever and make up for her tears.

Her voice echoed between my ears. My name over and over and over. Tears rolled off her words. Sobs cut the syllables in two.

A firm hand clasped my shoulder. "Yo, Second," Anderson said. His face scrunched. "Did you not sleep at all? You look like a zombie."

I shrugged. "I took the challenge very seriously."

He scoffed. "You *and* the other boys."

"No, I'm fine!" Huerta yelled, mid yawn. "I went to bed earlier than Glover and Second."

Glover violently zipped his backpack. Eyes locked on me with the flashlight in his grip. His weapon against me. After last night, he learned it cut me deeper than any blade. He doesn't care how much it hurts.

"Geez, he's cranky," Anderson whispered. His eyes darted toward a dark cloud approaching the mountaintop. He clicked his tongue. "We might have to be fast today. Probably gonna be another rough storm."

I nodded. "Let's play it safe. I don't want another accident."

"Captain Secoooooooonnd," Huerta whined. Metal clanks of a mug against bark resounded in an uneven rhythm. "I need coffee."

I shook my head and smiled. I was their camp counselor. I needed to cheer up. I needed to be there for them.

You weren't there for her.

The voice in my head taunted and twisted my heart.

I know I wasn't there for her.

I know she needed me.

I *will* make it up to her. I won't let this go unspoken. Not like last time. Never again.

10:03 AM

I hear her.

She's crying for me.

She's cursing my name.

"Second, you promised."

"Second, where are you?"

"Second, I thought you were different."

"I thought you were him."

Each word is a knife in my heart. Each word is a flash of light to bring me back to the night that haunts my soul.

I thought she would be the one to help me get over the pain I feel when I see lights. When the sun rays shine too bright. I thought she would be my new memory.

Now, her words cut deeper than the glass that followed the bright lights *that* night.

1:04 PM

I couldn't take it anymore. I couldn't take her sorrow. I couldn't take the memories surfacing with every painful cry.

Would I have to explain myself? Absolutely. Would I tell them what was really happening? Not likely. I'd rather they think I was crazy than tell them the truth.

"Captain Anderson, can we take a break," Hart called. His butt crashed too hard against his rock perch. He moaned and rubbed his back. "I'm tired."

Anderson laughed and leaned against a tree for support. "Whatsamattah, I thought none of you were tired?"

Cline's chest heaved. "It's easier going down than up." He shook out his feet. "But our legs are working harder to keep us from toppling forward."

"Thank you, Captain Obvious," Atkins mocked.

Pierce plopped down in the dirt and pulled a granola bar out of his backpack.

Sweeney kneeled down beside him, snapping a photo of the action.

I looked away before the flash went off.

Huerta laced his fingers behind his head. "I could use some lunch now. And maybe more coffee?"

"No more coffee," I snapped. I didn't mean to sound so harsh. Too many thoughts rushed through the rivers of my mind. The undertow swept half of them away. "I mean, we can't make a fire right now."

"Why don't you just eat the grinds?" Pierce said with his mouth full.

I pulled my backpack away from Huerta's reaching hands. "Don't encourage him."

"But I will die without the coffee," Huerta whined. He lurched forward. "We don't need a zombie *and* a ghost in these woods."

Glover's gaze melted the back of my head. My mind throbbed. We shouldn't *have* a ghost in the woods. GG needed to go home. To live peacefully in Heaven where she belonged.

I was supposed to send her there. I failed. She was meant to pass on. To escape her toxic ghost boyfriend.

Now, she's wandering the woods, cursing his name and mine.

"Captain Second, please?" Huerta begged, snapping me back into reality. "I need the coffee."

"You had some this morning." I did give him decaf again hoping the placebo would be enough. It worked for a little bit. "We need to save the rest for our last day tomorrow."

Huerta groaned and collapsed into the dirt. He grumbled a string of complaints in Spanish. Something he'd never done before.

Atkins scooted next to him. "I'll give you something that works better than coffee."

Huerta stopped mumbling and tilted his head. "I'm listening."

He pulled out a plastic container. "This is caffeinated gum." He popped out a white circle speckled with blue. "They give them to athletes before races to jump-start their heart. It has as much caffeine as a shot of espresso." Atkins winked at me.

I played along. "Espresso is stronger than Chef Jeff's coffee. I don't know if that's a good idea."

Huerta shoved two in his mouth.

"Atkins, I don't think you understand the consequences of your actions." Anderson said.

"I think we'll get down the mountain much faster now." Atkins smirked. "Especially if we wanna beat this storm." His index finger pointed up.

The dark cloud following us crept closer.

"Well, at least eat something with that caffeine." Anderson yanked snacks out of his pack. "We'll take a quick break and then keep moving. Gotta stay ahead of the rain."

While the other boys sat, I paced back and forth. GG hadn't spoken since the last break.

Was she okay? Had she gone?

Did she move on?

The thought brought momentary relief. Then, I missed her. I wanted to see her. I wanted to hear her say it was thanks to me that she was saved.

I wanted to save her.

But Glover's animosity prevented me from doing so.

I looked over my shoulder to see him sitting next to Huerta. His grip tightened around the flashlight. His defense against me.

I needed to talk to him. I needed to understand him. I promised I'd earn his name. But with every passing moment, I was further away from that reward. He hated me for some reason. I didn't do anything. He despised me ever since the first day of camp. He mocked my scars. He taunted my pain.

Stop, Second. You can't let it get to you.

I shook my head hard. I would not let it hurt me. I decided to explain myself to Glover. Talk things out. Give him a reason to trust me.

I stepped forward, but a voice stopped me:

"*Second. I've done something I regret.*"

My heart pounded in my chest. No. No. No. Only pain follows a sentence like that. I glanced over my shoulder. A light gleamed in the distance like the sun off a coin. It was her. I was certain of it.

I looked to Glover and then back into the woods. My camper or a ghost? Someone I was physically responsible for? Or someone I felt emotionally responsible for?

I ran with my emotions, praying I wouldn't regret it.

It was too late to realize I'm a hypocrite.

1:50 PM

"Second, Second, Second."

My nickname cut through the woods like a machete. It tore through the leaves and penetrated my heart. Sorrow laced each syllable. Tears choked each letter.

"I'm coming!" I didn't think how far away I was from the others. I told Anderson I'd be right back who hopefully assumed nature called.

Rolling clouds obstructed the sun like an eclipse. Boisterous thunder rumbled in the distance. Water droplets pattered against the stones like horses trampling across a field. Treetops thickened. Darkness blanketed the woods the further I went. I called for her again.

A light flashed to my right.

My ears rang and my chest ached. I skidded to a halt and squeezed my eye shut. Her appearance was too bright. Too fast.

"It's just her, Second, it's okay." I tried to stop myself before the pain returned.

Lights.

Glass.

Smoke.

Sirens.

Blood.

My chest heaved as I composed myself. The phantom copper taste of blood lingered on my tongue. The space behind my eyepatch throbbed.

I sucked in air through my teeth. "Second, it's just *her.*" My heart slowed and I ran into her clearing. The sounds of the forest muffled. The gentle rain did not follow me.

GG sat higher in her tree. Distant. Her chin tilted up. She shut her white eyes and kept her lips tight.

"I'm here, please." I scrambled over fallen logs and stood beneath her tree. "I don't know how long it's been, but I promise you. It was only a day, and I have a good explanation."

"You promised." Frozen words fell like icicles.

"I know, I didn't mean it."

"You told me to do this!" Her body flickered. "Then you leave me for almost a month."

My beating heart stopped. A fiery lump caught in my throat. A *month*? How did time work away from her? Did she approach the end of her time haunting earth? Was this the last stretch of her purgatory?

Or was her pain really my fault?

"I couldn't come visit you." I wrapped my arms around the trunk of her tree. "I had to take care of a kid."

"You had to take care of a kid. He had to take care of his reputation." She leaned over her branch. "Men and their excuses."

Beads of sweat trickled down my forehead. She compared me to him. The toxic ghost boyfriend. The one who probably *killed* her. My job was to change her past, having her breakup with him before her death.

"What did he do to you?" I could only muster six words. My imagination ran in twelve directions. Did he kill her like in Sparks's story? Was that why she was trapped in these woods?

"He told everyone I was crazy and then went berserk." Fists smashed into her legs. "He thought I *cheated* on him."

My heart pounded in my ears. "Why would he think that?" The bark scratched my stomach as I climbed up to her.

My hands gripped her branch when she stood up. Her blind eyes met mine. Glistening teardrops traced her face. "Because of *you*." She leaped off her tree. Her dress billowed around her. A ring of light rippled when she landed like a stone thrown in water.

Muscles burning, I descended the tree. "How is it my fault?" I didn't mean to sound accusatory. My confusion was genuine. I gave her advice on how to break up with her boyfriend so she could move on to heaven.

The worst I did was fall in love with her.

She scoffed. Hair floated wildly around her face. "How is it *your* fault?" Her body whipped around to face me. "You finally show up after ten years of writing to you. You tell me things I only prayed to hear. You give me the most honest advice I've heard. One that resonates with what my heart has been telling me."

Everything but my lips was paralyzed. "Your list sounds like all good things I've done."

"They are, *stupid.*" Her nose scrunched, and she stormed towards me. "You don't get it, do you?"

Butterflies fluttered in my stomach as she stood an inch from me. They weren't having a party. They panicked, wondering how they could make the situation better. A beautiful bright face painted with sadness stared into my soul.

I inhaled the scent of lavender and pine. My lips lingered inches from her forehead. Could I kiss her pain away? Could I wrap a hand around her waist and hold her against me, promising no one would hurt her again?

"Please, tell me what I don't get." My voice was small. "Why do those things hurt you?"

"You are an idiot." Her lip quivered. "I've waited for years." Anger melted into sadness. "And I've loved you since the beginning."

A hundred volts of lightning shot through my veins. Frantic beats threw my heart out of rhythm. The butterflies in my stomach partied and panicked. She didn't know my name. She didn't know what I looked like. She didn't know my past.

And she loved me anyway?

My cheeks burned. My chest ached. My mouth dried. "Y-you have?"

She dodged my question. "I told my boyfriend that I had found someone better. I couldn't tell him the truth… but withholding it didn't do me any good."

This wasn't supposed to happen. I fell in love with her because she paid attention to me. She was kind, caring, funny, sweet, understanding. She didn't dismiss my feelings. She wanted to know more about me, but I kept myself in a box. I dangled the key in front of her, but she didn't want to stop until she knew everything.

She was *not* supposed to love me. She was supposed to move on. To head to heaven where she didn't have to be alone anymore.

Did I ruin that chance?

"I-I don't know what to say." The truth.

"How about an apology?" Heat shot from her words. "Step off your high horse and *apologize.*"

My heart shattered. Didn't she know how sorry I was? I wrote "sorry" dozens of times in my journal when I couldn't run to her. Every moment she cried for me. Every time she screamed my name. I could only mutter one word.

But if she didn't know, it didn't matter.

I took a deep breath. Three words could cut ties to the heaviest weight. I prayed they would slice her burdens in two. "I am sorry."

Her shoulders relaxed. Tears like stars trickled down her transparent cheeks.

How could someone be so beautiful when they cried?

I lifted a hand. Fingers trembling, I reached for her cheek. I needed her to know I was there. I needed to *touch* her. I wondered if she'd feel human. Perhaps warm like the sun? My fingers hovered by her skin. I steeled myself for anything to happen. Would I pass right through her? She couldn't see me, but could she feel me?

My shirt tugged tightly around my neck. I gasped. Something yanked me backward.

Time slowed as I fell.

My right hand shot out and I grabbed her arm. My palm slid down it. A burning sensation shot from fingertips to wrist. An addictive sensation I craved. My skin tingled and I wanted to feel her again.

But as my body toppled backwards, I fell further and further away from her. I felt like I submerged in water, drowning as I clawed for the surface.

I didn't want to leave. I needed to tell her how I felt. I needed to tell her all I wanted to do was save her.

I needed to tell her that I loved her, too.

But only one word floated slowly from my lips: "Wait."

My vision blurred, but her voice rang clear. "I've been waiting long enough." She pressed the sides of her hands together. "Come find me." She clapped.

Her light vanished.

2:53 PM

Pain shot up from my butt to my head. Raindrops beat against my skull like sticks to a drum. Heat seared my hand.

I looked down to see a clean line of blood followed the lines in my palm. It burned like a paper cut. It ached, throbbed. The red liquid pricked a memory, but I forced it back.

I needed Ghost Girl back.

"You didn't even notice me, did you?" a voice shouted over the wind.

I pressed my palm against my light blue shirt and scrambled to my feet.

Glover stared at me with a flashlight tight in his grip. His brow furrowed. Wet bangs clung to his forehead, covering his dark eyes. Red dripped from his elbows down his forearms. "Why were you staring at nothing like a psycho?"

I glanced down at my watch. 2:53.

I was with her for an *hour*.

"Glover, I can explain," I cried.

The sky opened further and the rain crashed down violently. Loud and strong like an army of Vikings beating against their shields before battle.

I spit water out of my mouth and shouted over the noise. "Let's get to shelter before we get drenched."

"Too late!" Glover held his arms out, welcoming the downpour. "Tell me now. Don't make me use this." He flickered the flashlight.

Lights.

No. I pushed the memory away. "Why don't you explain yourself first. Why are you so concerned with what I do? So what if I'm crazy and stare at trees for hours."

He waved the flashlight at my feet.

Lights.

No.

I pinched my eye shut and shook my head. I wouldn't let it win. "After camp, you won't see me. Why do you care about what I do?"

"Maybe because the captains of Southpaw are supposed to help?"

He took a step closer. "And you promised."

I cocked my head. "What does me being in the woods have to do with my promise?"

Glover's knuckles turned white. "Do you want to know?"

My wet shirt clung to my frame. "Yes!"

"I can't trust you anymore!" His voice cracked. Tears raced with the raindrops sliding down his cheeks. "You tell me to talk about my feelings? Well, why don't you tell me the truth instead of hiding in the woods for some prank." He threw the flashlight down. It shattered against the stone. "You got to know the other boys! Why do you keep running away to some 'ghost' when it's time to get to know me?"

Rain beat harder against the forest. I paused for a minute, drinking in his words. Glover cried for help. He yearned for attention. He begged for someone to listen to him before something bad happened.

Just like I had done years ago.

Glover covered his mouth with trembling hands. "Guys aren't supposed to cry." Red veins spread across his eyes. "Then why do I want to all the time?"

My heart beat in my ears. "Glover, I—"

A flash of lightning cracked against the sky. The entire forest lit up.

A scream crawled up my throat.

Every memory flooded back with the downpour.

5 Years Ago

She hit me.

It didn't hurt. They said she was just playing.

She insulted me. Called me names.

She was just flirting. She didn't mean it.

She put me down when we were out with friends.

She was just being funny. Learn to take a joke.

She yelled at me if I was late to reply.

She was lonely. Stop being so inconsiderate.

She forced herself upon me even if I said no.

She wants love. Stop being so selfish.

She talked with some other guys behind my back.

She was just making friends. No need to get upset.

She cursed and punched me when I told her I needed a break.

She was heartbroken and it was my fault. I couldn't cry, I needed to man up.

She crashed the car with me in it after I broke up with her.

It was okay to cry now. Even though tears would only fall from one eye.

DAY 5 OF THE HIKING TRIP

3:03 PM

Glover's screaming brought me out of my thoughts. My heart beat loud in my ears. The sounds of the rain resumed.

I sat on the ground. Body drenched, cold and quaking. My eye darted back and forth. The woods of Camp Southpaw.

I'm not in the car. I'm not in the car, I thought over and over.

My body shook again. Jaw clenched, I blinked several times. I couldn't see. Why couldn't I see?

Glover's fingers wrapped tightly around my arms. "Captain Second!"

I watched his figure blur in my vision. Then, I realized why nothing was clear.

Tears flooded my only eye.

"Guys aren't supposed to cry." Glover's words boiled the water streaming down my cheek. Every tear burned. I tried to stop, but the dam burst.

"G-glover." My chest rose and fell rapidly. I pressed my bleeding hand over my heart. "What happened?"

"A crack of lightning and then you *ducking* fell over." He kneeled beside me. The flashlight stuck in the mud. "I'm not asking. *Tell me what happened?*"

I wiped my palm across my eye. I stared at Glover's face, searching for the meaning behind his words.

Worry. Fear. Pain. All three contorted his youthful features. Glover felt genuinely concerned for me.

"I want the truth," Glover demanded.

My lips parted, then closed. The rain washed over us, soaking every layer of clothing. The blood trickled down my palm and mixed with the mud. I'd take suffering in the rain over telling him the truth. I'd welcome hypothermia if it meant my secret stayed with me.

"You told me it's okay for guys to have feelings," Glover said. "I think you're being hypocritical right now."

I was. I knew the answer. I knew how to fix every other boy's problems. I knew how to fix my own.

"*Sharing pain with someone who understands is the first step to mending a heart.*"

Ghost Girl told me that. She gave me the answer. She gave me every opportunity, and I blew it. I caused her grief. I left her when she needed me. She needed to share her pain to mend her heart. She wanted me to share so she knew she wasn't alone. She deserved an apology.

But, now she's gone.

I took a shaky breath. It was time. It was time I told someone. I *ducked* up with Ghost Girl. I didn't open up in time. I wouldn't make that mistake twice.

Besides: Glover needed me. He needed someone to be truthful. He needed someone to relate to.

I promised to earn his name. First, I needed his trust.

The wind slowed and the rain quieted. I shared a story I tucked away on the shelf of my heart. Hidden. Never to be read. Now, I pulled it off the bookcase and poured over the pages.

I tore a piece of my shirt and bandaged my palm. "If you couldn't tell, I don't like bright lights. Accompanied by loud noises?" I shook my head and clicked my tongue. "I can't control my thoughts. They go back to the day I…" I inhaled through my nose. "I lost my eye." I exhaled. My racing heart did not explode, so I continued. "My ex-girlfriend was toxic. Nobody saw it but me. Nobody listened until it was too late. She was controlling and wanted to drive us back from a date that night. The night I told her I needed a break. She didn't like that." The feeling of a seatbelt pressed against my chest. "She freaked out, screaming at me. 'You're selfish. You hate me. You'll never find anyone else.' Those sorts of things." I rubbed my shoulder. "She hit me repeatedly while we drove, not paying attention." I bit my tongue and closed my eyes. I didn't want to say it. I didn't want to continue.

Water welled in my eye. The one preserved from the glass of the windshield. The one that watched her bleeding body go limp over the steering wheel. The one that wept when the sirens sounded.

The sky dried, but my eye did not. It continued to rain as my chest heaved. My lips sealed. My heart thumped. No more. I could not take more.

Warmth enveloped my frigid, quaking body. A gentle pressure squeezed my arms. I opened my eye.

Glover hugged me. He bent over my broken soul and held it together. The boy that hated to be touched because of pain from home. A boy I wanted to help.

He helped me instead. Even if it hurt him.

I wrapped my arms around him and let my tear duct drain. "I am sorry, Glover." My voice cracked.

"Dude, why are you sorry?" He sounded offended. "You are the first dude I've ever seen cry. I thought I would feel awkward, but," he sighed, "I actually feel relieved."

I laughed and pulled away. "Relieved? I guess that's good."

"No duh, idiot." Glover sat back onto a rock. "I was intimidated by how cool and manly you were. Seeing you cry shows me you're not a camp counselor robot or something."

I snorted. "Me? Manly?"

"Dude, you have a thick *brass* beard, can carry the hiking packs of three campers, pulled off the most epic prank of Southpaw without getting in trouble, and," he tapped my eyebrow, "you look like a *ducking* pirate."

I laughed. "I'm honored."

"You should be." Glover crossed his arms. "I never usually admit what I really think of anyone. You're the first."

My eyebrows raised. For a moment, I was speechless. Kind words from a broken soul meant more than a hundred compliments. "And you're the first person I told the real reason why I wear an eyepatch."

Glover's eyes widened. "I'll remember that." He clicked his tongue. "Now, the ghost?"

I exhaled through my nose. "She's real."

He nodded but said nothing else. His eyes locked with mine. His gaze wasn't harsh like the nights I snuck away. They were soft. Understanding.

I got to my feet. Mud stuck in every crack. A chill crawled across my damp skin. Thankfully, the sun poked through the clouds. I prayed we'd dry.

"We should probably get back." I stuck out a hand.

Glover stared at it for a moment. He grabbed it and let me help him to his feet. He didn't let go right away. With a smile, he said, "My first name is Caleb."

Five words warmed my soul. That was all I wanted to know. I would cherish his trust and never let him down again.

"Nice to meet you, Caleb."

4:00 PM

"Guys don't have feelings."

"Guys aren't supposed to cry."

Myths. Lies. I can be a man and still have emotions. Men aren't stupid stoic creatures like everyone made me believe in high school.

I can't believe it took a ghost and a cub to make me realize the truth.

As we made our way back, we chatted as if nothing ever happened. He didn't see me have a breakdown. I didn't pour my heart out to him. We were a counselor and a camper trekking through the woods, joking about mud being stuck in all the wrong places.

Echoing shouts overlapped between the trees. "Second! Glover!"

We ran towards the clamor. Anderson stood atop a rock with the eleven cubs yelling for us around him.

"Anderson, we're good!" I waved.

The captain's eyes widened and he jumped off his rock. "Where the *bells* have you been?"

"We went for a walk and tried to wait out the storm, but clearly…" I tugged on my darkened, torn blue shirt.

Anderson pointed to my wrapped palm. "How'd that happen?"

"We slipped." Glover showed off his raw elbows. "That's what happens when water covers the ground."

Anderson rolled his eyes. "Not funny, guys. Scared the *ducking bells* out of me." He jammed a thumb over his shoulder. "I radioed camp. They're coming to get us."

I tilted my head. "We've survived thunderstorms before."

Anderson threw his arms out. "Well, Huerta made me panic so I called camp to pick us up. We couldn't find you, the rain got harder, lots of lightning, he said he heard you both scream, whatever. I didn't want to take chances."

Huerta jumped up and stood behind Anderson. "Look, the ghost is angry at us." He grabbed my co-captain's arms and peered around. "Her tears rained from the sky." His eyes darted toward me. "Did you make her upset?"

Glover and I exchanged glances.

Why hide it anymore? Half of the Cubs believed Huerta's dramatic retelling of Sparks' story. Half still thought I played along.

Regardless, there was no judgment. No risk in telling the truth.

I let out a long sigh. "Yeah, I made the ghost upset. I promised I'd be there for her, but I wasn't."

Two sentences released a hundred weights chained to my wrists. The truth, no matter who believed it, felt better to say than beating around the bush. Was the whole situation crazy? Yeah. Could this be a story from a fiction novel? Absolutely. But it ended up being my life.

I fell in love with a ghost. And then, I broke her heart.

Huerta clicked his tongue. "You hear that? Captain Second failed to keep the ghost at bay. She will forever haunt these woods." He slumped away. "Why must we be tortured?"

Anderson shakes his head. "If you don't find this Ghost Girl and apologize, he's gonna be miserable for the rest of the session."

My heart sank. Huerta wouldn't be the only one miserable. I wanted to apologize. I wanted her to know all I wanted to do was send her home. To give her peace.

But I made her afterlife worse.

I felt Glover's eyes on me. Not judgmental. Not hateful. Sympathetic. He was the only one to know she was real; to know that I didn't disappear from camp for no reason.

I felt responsible for Ghost Girl. No. I *wanted* to be responsible for her. I wanted to take care of her. I wanted to be the one to save her and send her home. Turns out I needed to be saved from myself.

She saved me. Glover saved me.

Huerta wailed dramatically. He whined and stomped back and forth, splashing mud on the other cubs. "We must find her and toss Second at her, begging for forgiveness." He sank to his knees. Brown stained his khaki cargo shorts. "Let her return to God and leave Southpaw in peace!"

"All right, that's enough." Pierce yanked Huerta to his feet.

"Your acting is not improving. It's just getting more annoying." Glover quipped.

Huerta pouted. "C'mon, man. You gotta be dramatic with a story like this." He threw his arms out. "When someone retells our story to the next campers, there has to be something more than walking, trees, talking, and campfires."

"That would make a boring book or movie." Atkins snorted.

"Which is why *I* need to be dramatic." Huerta flipped his hair. "I will not have my fans be bored."

"Well, no one will tell our story unless we get off the mountain." I looked around. "Did you guys grab my bag?"

Sweeney raised his hand. His round eyes sparkled. A small smile spread across his lips.

I went over and retrieved it. "What are you smirking about?"

Sweeney shook his head. In his grip was a plastic bag that protected his instant-print camera. "You'll see."

I never liked that answer but exhaustion stopped me from pressing further. The chill of my damp clothing crept across my skin. While I hated bailing early on a hike, I didn't want to go home next week with the flu.

A rumbling shook the mountain. Huerta dropped into the mud and cried out, "Forgive us, Ghost Girl! Take Captain Second as a sacrifice!"

Atkins dropped down next to him while the rest of the cubs shouted for Huerta to shut up.

Four all-terrain vehicles traversed into the mountain clearing. Director Carter hopped out of the driver's side. Brow furrowed, his eyes darted from each camper. "Are you boys okay? Where are the two that were lost?"

"We're right here." I stood beside Glover and raised my hand.

Director Carter exhaled. "Thank goodness. I was about to call in the chopper."

"Wait, I want to fly in a helicopter," Cline exclaimed.

Fischer pointed behind him. "What if we go hide in the woods? Can we call it to come get us?"

The director shook his head. "No free rides today, boys. Now, let's get back to camp and get you into dry clothes."

The boys piled in each car by threes and fours. I sat with Glover, Sweeney, and Director Carter. The ATV jerked and shook with each rock and pebble on the path. The hum of the engine didn't stop me from keeping an ear to the woods.

I prayed to hear her. I prayed to see her. I prayed to get the chance to apologize.

But the further we descended, the farther away she felt.

6:04 PM

I will never take clean clothes for granted. My musty white shirt felt like a heated blanket against my chilled skin. I will also never take soup for granted—especially not breakfast soup (so they called it). I slurped the creamy orange liquid. The sweetness of yams and apples sat on my tongue. My body rejuvenated, but my heart still felt cold.

Ghost Girl hated me, but I loved her. I believed I failed her. Would she ever be at peace? Or would she find another forest to roam until someone could save her?

I sat beside Glover and watched as the other cabins approached our table to ask what happened. Huerta and Atkins gave their dramatic retelling. Sweeney took instant photos of the campers who came over and asked questions. Now everyone at Camp Southpaw knew about Captain Second and the Ghost Girl.

"You're even more popular now," Cline said. "You even have photographic evidence of your fan club."

"They're all believers now." Atkins butted in. He shook a photo as it developed. "Cline, have you finally accepted the truth?"

"For a nerd, you should have eaten this stuff up," Huerta joked.

Cline stuck out his tongue and proceeded to pick the parsley out of his breakfast soup.

Sparks and Bancroft from Pack Coyote slid down the wooden bench to sit beside Anderson and me. "If it isn't the Ghost Lover," Sparks whispered into my ear. "How is your girlfriend?"

"Gone, weren't you listening?" I slurped the final drop of my soup. My soul remained icy. My heart ached and my head hurt. "I failed her and now she hates me."

Anderson arched an eyebrow. "I'm starting to wonder if this Ghost Girl is supposed to be someone else."

Sparks shot him a look. "*Cletus*, Anderson, just play along," he whispered. "The cubs all think I'm a spirit whisperer. It's gonna make next year *ducking* exciting for me since you two are too old to come back unless the director chooses you especially."

Anderson rolled his eyes and threw up his hands.

Bancroft pulled out his puzzle cube. He twisted it twice backwards and placed it in front of me; incomplete. Crossing his arms, he leaned back and jerked his chin towards the cube.

I took Bancroft's prized possession into my calloused hands. In the four years that I've worked at Camp Southpaw, I never touched his cube. I tightened the bandage around my palm, then twisted it forward twice. They lined up, each face now a solid color. "Yay, I did it." I said sarcastically.

Bancroft took the cube back and twisted it back three times. He placed it in front of me, then I fixed it again. He did it again with four twists. I fixed it *again*.

After the fifth time, I said, "Okay, Bancroft, what's up? You never let anyone play with your toy."

He arched an eyebrow. "Play? You're solving a problem to make the final picture." His fingers flew like lightning, mixing up the colors. "We mess up. Mix up the colors. It's chaotic and doesn't make sense. But with a little effort and perseverance—" He twisted it and in seconds he solved it. "You can put everything back into place."

I blinked three times. Even though Bancroft preferred silence, wisdom flowed from his lips every time he spoke. However this time, I couldn't tell if his words were inspirational or nonsensical.

Sparks tried to interpret his analogy. "Basically, Second shouldn't give up even though he keeps messing up." He patted my back. "Your campers need you. Don't look so defeated."

I looked down the table at the boys. They chatted amongst themselves with grins on their faces. These boys poured their hearts out to me over the past week. They have grown as young men under my direction.

I glanced over at Glover. His smile spread ear to ear as he flung green parsley at Cline. He laughed with the boys. He looked *happy*.

Did I fail Ghost Girl? Yes. But these boys? They still needed me. Sure, I messed up the "colors" of my life. There are six sides to the cube and you can only solve one side at a time. I just have to keep going until everything is in place.

I messed up with Ghost Girl. Do I believe she was real? Absolutely. Whether she was a real paranormal spirit or something in my head, she related to someone I felt called to take care of. To love and cherish. Maybe one day, I'll meet the real her. I'll meet the woman I will be responsible for. The woman I'll say "I love you" to every night.

But for now, I'll solve one side at a time. I thought the first one would be helping these boys. It turns out, the first one was helping myself.

As long as I keep going, all the colors will twist into place.

August 10

7:02 AM

August 11

I didn't write yesterday. I spent time being present rather than going off somewhere to document about my day. I took my time with the boys. My heart still clung to Ghost Girl, but I needed to rest. I needed to unplug from my own thoughts. No worrying about who said what when. No worrying about overthinking. Just being in the moment with my campers. We bet pieces of sausage at breakfast, played games with Pack Coyote, snacked on trail mix, and talked around the campfire.

Next: time to say goodbye.

I stood in the center of the cabin. Bunk beds to my left, right, and in front. Each boy sat atop their respective mattress, begrudgingly packing their belongings. None of them wanted to go home. They overstuffed their suitcases and duffel bags with unfolded laundry.

"This was the best year at Camp Southpaw," Huerta exclaimed. He shoved his underpants into the front pocket of his backpack. "We almost died multiple times, there was a confirmed ghost sighting, *and* we spent the last day just *ducking* around."

"Sounds like what you do normally." Glover snorted.

Pierce laughed and placed the last folded shirt into his bag. He had his tish together. "You're not wrong. He always gets me in trouble after school."

"Ugh, don't even talk about school yet," Atkins groaned. He elbowed his suitcase to get it shut. "I'm not ready to go back."

"Things will be better this year." Cline zipped up his superhero suitcase. "Just play lacrosse for fun and do all the nerdy ghost research you want."

Atkins grinned. "Thanks, man, I'll try."

Glover groaned. "Ugh, let's not get sentimental or talk about how much better we feel because of camp."

His tone said sarcasm, but his eyes said otherwise. Our unspoken connection strengthened. I felt how this past week had changed him. He needed time away more than an employee needed vacation. He had needed a retreat to reflect. That's what he received.

But what would happen to Glover when he went back? He never spoke of how difficult home life was. He never disclosed why he feared being touched. Although, the signs are obvious…

I was not going to let him go alone. While I would never be able to impact him like I did this past week, I could at least offer to be there when he needed me most. When *any* of the boys needed me most.

I sat beside Pierce; his bunk squeaked beneath my weight. I tore a few pages out of the back of my journal. "Well, when the camp-high fades away." I scribbled my phone number onto six torn pieces. "You can always text me if you want."

Huerta snagged a piece first. "You're *ducking* right I'll be in touch." He shoved it into the same pocket of his backpack as his underwear. "I need to know immediately if you see Ghost Girl again."

Atkins took my number next. "Ditto. I'm knee deep in this ghost story."

"Glad you're already taking my advice about taking care of your nerdy self," Cline took my number and slid it into his glasses case. "I'm sure I'll reach out with other wilderness questions."

"Pierce, take his number," Huerta commanded. "I'll need a backup copy in case I lose mine."

Pierce rolled his eyes. "I was going to take it anyway. I think having Captain Second on speed dial is a flex."

Huerta nodded. "Exactly! Like when his story hits TV, we can call him up to buy us all a cool car or have us all live in a mansion."

I laughed. "I don't think I'll get famous from this ghost story. I might be able to get you t-shirts or something."

Glover rose from his bed and swung his arms. "Well, I'd rather have a car, but—" He took the second-to-last piece. "I guess a free t-shirt is good enough to contact you." His grin brightened his eyes.

His contagious smile brought me joy. He took my contact info with our silent understanding of "if you need anything." I prayed our conversations would not have to be serious. I hoped he (and the other boys) would reach out to catch up. But if they were troubled and going through a challenging time, I prayed they would reach out, too.

I want to be the man for these boys I had wished someone was for me.

"I have one left." I waved the paper. "Sweeney, what's wrong? You don't want to talk to me anymore?"

Sweeney chuckled. Red flushed his round cheeks. The bunk shook when he stood up. Hands hid behind his back.

"What are you hiding, dude?" Huerta snorted.

"A gift." Sweeney jerked his chin at me. "You have to take it or I won't take your number."

"I don't know if that threat will work." Glover scoffed.

"No, no, I think it's a fair deal." I stretched out my hand. "Besides, I love gifts."

Sweeney smiled. He placed a small bulging envelope on my palm. The flap opened slightly. String wrapped tightly around it to keep it from tearing.

"Did you wrap up a rock?" Atkins joked.

Sweeney took the paper with my number and shook his head. "He'll see."

I shook the envelope gently. The contents rustled and shifted. Gently, I tugged on the string. Peeling back the flap, I looked inside to see a stack of instant-print photos.

"Whoa, cool!" I pulled out the first. It was an overexposed photo of Anderson and I when we first introduced ourselves outside the Handcraft Cabin. Another was from our first campfire night. "Are these all the photos you took?"

He shrugged. "I kept a few for myself, and I made sure everyone got one. But we agreed that you should have the most."

My eye jumped from face to face. "Why did you want me to have them all?"

"Well, we know how many campers you have during the summer."

Huerta shrugged. "We'll never forget you, but we want to make sure you never forget us."

"Also, we figured you could put them in your journal," Cline added.

Warmth spread across my cheeks. "Wow, thanks, guys. I'll definitely put them between the pages." I started to pull them out of the envelope.

"Wait until you get back home," Sweeney exclaimed. His face became a tomato. "J-just because it'll be better to remember the memories."

I smirked and tucked them back into their envelope. "Yes, sir."

Anderson ran up the cabin steps and knocked on the doorframe. "You guys ready for our Pack Cottontail group photo?"

The boys dropped their bags onto their bunks and followed Anderson and me out. We crossed the fields and stood beneath the flagpole at the center of camp where Sparks' underwear flew a few days ago.

The wind blew through my hair. I inhaled deeply; the scent of lake water filled my lungs. We shuffled into a line with the rest of Pack Cottontail. Anderson and I stood at either end while the boys stood in a line between us.

Pack Coyote was in charge of our group photo. Sparks held the camera up to his eye and started a finger countdown. The shutter clicked and we switched poses.

The group photo always marked the end of a session. Now, it marked the end of the summer. I couldn't believe it was over. The boys of Pack Cottontail would return to their normal lives, go back to school, and fall into a regular routine.

If it was a normal session, I'd be more worried about the boys. I'd be worried they would forget everything they learned and the friends they made.

But this group? I'm not worried at all.

They've all grown so much over the past week. I was blessed to be a part of that journey. Sure, we faced thunderstorms, almost slid down a cliff, and encountered a ghost, but everything happened for a reason. Whether I saw it this week or not, I know they've all changed for the better.

And frankly, so have I.

12:03 PM

Glover was the last one to be picked up. He and I sat in the dining hall with Anderson, Sparks, and Bancroft.

Glover, Anderson, and I slid a paper cup back and forth across the mahogany table. It glided along like a ghost. Like Ghost Girl. I thought of every encounter we had. Her anti-gravity hair, her curvy figure, her adorable laugh. Gah, her laugh.

Her last words replayed in my head. "*Come find me.*" How? How do you track down a ghost?

The cup slid too far out of my reach. It slid off the table.

I stifled a sigh. I bent over to pick it up and hit my head on the table. "Gah, *mama duck.*" I swore.

Sparks laughed. "You'll be off duty soon. You can use the real words."

I rubbed my head. "Whatever, dude." The bandage got caught in my hair. I peeled it off. Nothing was going my way.

Glover's eyes darted to my hand. His lips formed a straight line. He was the only one to know where the gash across my palm came from. The only one who knew she was real.

Glover cleared his throat. "Captain Sparks, can I ask you something?"

He laughed. "So polite. What's up?"

"Do you know anything about who the people are in your ghost story?"

"If you wanna go find the girl's body, it's no use." Sparks picked up a plastic spoon. He tapped the bottom along the table. "She walks these woods not knowing her name. Not knowing her identity. Trying to find a trace of who she was is impossible."

My heart sank. Perhaps if I knew her real name, I could call to her. I could ask her to come back or pray for her soul. To have closure knowing that maybe I made a difference… before I failed her.

"Are you *sure* no one knows her name?" Glover insisted.

Sparks scoffed. "Are you saying I'm a storyteller that's missed critical details?"

Bancroft laughed. "Yes." He spun his puzzle cube on the table.

"You would forget your own name if it wasn't in your contacts."

"Not true!"

Bancroft arched an eyebrow. "Okay, then tell me: which cousin invited you to that fancy gala next month that you kept bragging about to our cubs?"

Sparks growled. "I'm Irish-Catholic, okay? I have about at least a dozen cousins. Not remembering the name of one doesn't count."

Anderson laughed and took Spark's spoon. "I bless thee." My co-captain tapped Sparks's freckled forehead three times. Then three more times. Then again.

"Ugh, fine, so maybe I just forgot the ghost's name," Sparks admitted, ignoring Anderson tapping his face with the spoon. "What I can say is it *is* a true story."

My heavy heart lightened. "Well, if I'm going to be famous for meeting the ghost, I think I need to figure out her name."

"You probably just want to see her again." Anderson made kissing noises.

I punched Anderson's arm. "I don't think anyone can kiss a ghost." I definitely wished, though…

"I'm sure some weird ghost-nerds like Atkins think you can." Glover snorted.

"Speaking of ghost nerds." Sparks tapped the side of his face. "I *do* remember that it was one of my cousins who told me the story. Not the cousin who invited me to the gala." He shot a glance at Bancroft who shrugged. "She could probably recite the original. " Sparks chuckled and fiddled with a string on his pants. "I also think the story is about her mom's sister's cousin or whatever. I don't know the connection."

My lightened heart started to flutter. "Can you ask her?"

"Second, you should've first called him out for being a thief," Anderson teased. "Then, you should've called him out for making light of a family member's trauma."

"Shut up, dude," Sparks snapped. "But yeah, man, I'll ask my dad. He'll remind me who told us the story. Definitely one of his brother's kids."

"Do you remember who your dad is?" Bancroft taunted.

Sparks rolled his eyes. "Ha. Ha. Very funny. I may be forgetful, but I'm not *that* forgetful."

Bancroft smirked. "What's your uncle's name?"

Sparks laughed sarcastically and took the spoon back from Anderson before he was "blessed" an eighteenth time.

A phone vibrated. Glover pulled out his broken smartphone and answered the call. "Y-yeah, I'll be right out." He stammered. Rising to his feet, he slung his bag over his shoulder. "That's my ride."

"I'll walk you to the parking lot." I stood, threw on my backpack, and ruffled Sparks's hair on my way out.

Glover and I walked in silence to the car. Sadness darkened his face. His feet dragged along the dirt.

I wanted to ask what was wrong at home. I wanted to make sure he would be okay. Camp Southpaw patched him up. I didn't want him to break all over again.

We stopped beneath the wooden archway. "CAMP SOUTHPAW" spelled in wooden letters hung across the top beam on both sides. To remind where you were as you entered, and where you came from returning to the real world.

I didn't want Glover to go back into the real world. But after how he handled me and Ghost Girl, I knew he could take care of himself. He's strong, but needs someone to lean on at times.

I lifted a hand to place it on his shoulder but refrained. Glover didn't like being touched. I looked into his dark eyes. "You contact me if you need anything."

Glover took a deep breath and nodded. He turned and began to walk toward the parking lot where his father sat in the car. Away from the safety of Camp Southpaw and back into the claws of society.

I wanted to shake his hand. Call out to him. Something. But through a dirty windshield, I saw his father's glare. I didn't want to get Glover in trouble.

Halfway to the car, Glover stopped. He slid his backpack off his shoulder and threw the duffel bag onto the ground. His shoulders raised and fell in time with his deep inhale.

Then, he turned and walked back toward me.

"Forget something?" I asked, looking down at him.

He's a half-foot shorter than I am, but he stood tall. His shoulders back.

He stuck out a hand. "Captain Second."

I grinned and grasped it.

Then, Glover pulled me in for a hug. His arms wrapped tight around me like they did back in the forest. Back when I needed him the most. When my past pain was too much to bear.

"Thank you for everything, Captain Second." Glover's voice shook. He squeezed harder, not wanting to let go.

Such a broken boy, frightened by the thought of being touched. Now, he rushed to me for a comforting hug. A hug he shouldn't be afraid to receive from anyone—especially not his parents.

But he came to me. I will not take it for granted.

"Caleb Glover," I patted his back, "you are stronger than you realize. You will do just fine."

He pulled away. Water welled in his eyes. He chuckled, wiping his cheek. "Thanks for teaching me that I can cry and still be cool."

I laughed. "Well, just don't do it all the time." I flexed dramatically. "You always gotta keep up a manly appearance."

"Well, I hope I never have to wear an eyepatch." He tapped his face. "But I'll try and grow up to be a man like you, someday."

A smile spread across my face. Before this past week, I never wanted any of the boys to be like me. To be afraid of their past. To fear for their future.

Now, I'm honored.

"You'll be a better man than me."

Glover's grin reached his eyes. He walked to pick up his things and continued to his car. He threw his bags in the pack and opened the passenger side door. Before sitting down, he looked at me and shouted, "I know you'll find her!" He winked and slid into his seat. In an instant, the car sped off.

I shoved my hands into my pockets. "I sure hope so, Glover." I made my way back across the campgrounds.

Everything was quiet. The remaining captains shuffled back and forth, checking cabins and cleaning the grounds. The wind blew a cool breeze off Lake Solid. I inhaled deeply. I tasted lake water and seaweed. No lavender and pine.

I prayed Glover was right. I prayed I would find Ghost Girl again.

The campfire pit was abandoned. Ashes scattered around the circle of stones. I stood beside it and stared into the woods. I wanted to see lights. Any little flicker of hope that she was still there. I wanted to see her again one last time.

With a sigh, I sat onto one of the log benches and flung my bag onto the ground. The flap opened and Sweeney's envelope slid out. Photographs scattered across the ground.

"Tish." I scooped them up, shaking the dirt off before placing them back into the envelope. I glanced at each one. Memories of breakfast, fluffy marshmallows, sticky buns, burning fires, capture the flag, and the views of the sunset.

I reached for the last photo, but a gust of wind blew it away. Securing my backpack's clasp, I swung the pack over my shoulder and chased after it.

The photo tumbled along the grass, taunting me. I extended my arm and snatched it before it crossed the border into the forest.

"Where do you think you're going?" I asked aloud. I flipped it over and looked closely at the photo.

My breath caught in my chest.

The forest was dark. Leaves hung over two figures in the center. The one on the left was me. Not hard to tell with my beard, eyepatch, and light-blue shirt. The figure on the right was impossible to misidentify. The white skin, white dress, white anti-gravity hair.

Ghost Girl.

A breeze blew from the woods. Lavender and pine floated along it, enveloping me. I breathed in the scent, filling my lungs. Never wanting to forget the joy it brought me.

I pressed the photograph to my lips. I failed her once. I prayed for a second chance. An opportunity to make it up to her and give her the peace she gave me in the moments we shared.

I laughed and looked into the woods. Darkness looked back at me.

"It is my turn to wait for you, Ghost Girl."

September 9

I missed camp more than usual this morning. I craved the rush of the morning wind on the mountain top. The glowing fires that warmed our tired bodies. The people I shared it with. The woman I wished for.

But I'm back in real life. However, nothing has been the same. I'm glad; I never wanted it to be.

My phone vibrated across my nightstand. I put aside my laptop and answered the phone call. "Yo?"

"Dude, I'm surprised you're awake." Sparks laughed. "You weren't answering the texts in the captain group chat."

"I'm working on my resume. A new job as an adjunct English Professor for my *alma mater* posted yesterday."

"Ugh, I feel like all you do is look for jobs."

I scoffed. "Not everyone is blessed to have a job handed down to them."

"Oh, shut up, dude."

"Now what did I do to be worthy of a phone call from you? Did you finally find me information on my Ghost Girl?" I had started calling her "mine" after we left Camp Southpaw. It seemed only fitting. If anyone helped find her, I wanted to set the precedent that I was the man in the story to save her.

"Actually, kind of. You down for a Southpaw Captain reunion?"
I smiled. "Always."

"Remember I talked about the cousin who knew the ghost story and the other one whose event I was invited to? Well, the ghost story one will be at the event with the other one!"

"Let me guess: they're siblings."

"Bingo! See? I'm remembering more. Now, my dad has extra tickets because my three youngest siblings are too little to come."

"So that means only four Sparks are going?"

"Yep. You down? It's tomorrow night. Wear formal."

I pretended to think. "Do I have to pay money? I'm out of a job right now."

"Nope. Ticket is paid for. It's a fundraising Gala for my cousin's company. She's running the whole thing. You coming or what? Anderson said I have permission to drag your ass if you say no."

I laughed. "Fine, fine. Just send me the address and I'll be there. Bye." I hung up and tossed my phone aside. I let out a deep breath and pulled out my journal. It had been about a month since Camp Southpaw ended. I didn't write in it as much. I would open the journal, look at the pictures I tucked between the pages, and replace it on my nightstand.

But any night with my co-captains is worth adding to my Southpaw journal.

Besides, if Sparks' cousin can help me find Ghost Girl, then I wanted to write down every detail.

I know I will find her. I can feel it.

September 10

8:05 PM

I felt like a homeless person crashing a wedding when I pulled up to the event in my beat-up SUV. I stepped out of the car and stared at the neo-Classical venue. Tall white pillars reached up to the marble arches. Colorful lights danced across the windows.

I dropped my keys into the valet-guy's hand and walked up the steps.

"Yo, Second!" Sparks waved me through the doorway. He wore a navy blue suit, white collared shirt, and tie. Everything complimented his light eyes and ginger hair. I never saw him so dressed up.

Sparks shook my hand and gave me a hug. "Glad you made it!"

I tugged on my light-blue tie. "I know you said formal but I didn't think it was this formal."

"My cousin works for some hot-shot entertainment company. This is to fundraise for their charity." He looked around, leaned in, and whispered, "She likes her job, but some of her co-workers are weird. Stay away from them."

I laughed. "No promises."

"Wassup, Second?"

I turned around to see Anderson and Bancroft approach carrying beers in each hand.

I took one from Anderson and clinked the necks of our bottles. "Always a pleasure, Captains."

Bancroft took a swig of his lager. "We scouted out the area."

"They're walking around with *amazing* appetizers." Anderson kissed his fingers. "Who knew chicken and waffle bites were considered fancy?"

"They sound sweet," I replied. "Bring me to them."

Sparks led the way into the ballroom. I picked my jaw up off the floor.

White tulle draped from the center of the high crystal chandeliers and out to each corner. Servants in tuxedos scurried back and forth with trays held above their heads. Men in suits and women in long gowns chatted. Their voices erupted like hundreds of seagulls squawking over Lake Solid.

Sparks elbowed me. "C'mon, guys, I'm starving."

The sweet aroma of syrup wafted past me. "I smell the waffles." I flagged down the servant and plucked six from the plate. I handed one to each of my friends and inhaled the rest.

Anderson gulped down the rest of his beer. "Dude, are we expected to donate anything to this charity?"

Sparks shrugged. "Only if you want to. My parents usually give something good. My siblings and I just got invited because one of my sisters is close with my cousin."

The corporate cousin sounded lovely, but I was more interested in the one who could help me find Ghost Girl. She was the reason I was here. Sure, I wanted to see the guys. They were a bonus. "And who is the cousin that you said I can meet to talk about the ghost story?"

Sparks clenched his teeth and frowned. "I told you she is the sister to my cousin running this."

"Do you really not know anyone's names?" Anderson scoffed.

Sparks scrunched his nose. "I'm not that forgetful. It's just more fun to be annoying. One name I definitely know is my sister's." He smacked his forehead. "Look, let's grab another drink, find my sister Brigid, and hide when they start asking for donations."

Bancroft shook his head and asked a servant beside us for a stronger drink than beer.

Anderson asked for the same.

So did Sparks.

And so did I.

9:10 PM

Drinking bourbon mixed with soda and searching through 450 guests in a fancy mansion is not smart. I ended up networking with some of the donors at the gala. I was told I'm "personable" and "have potential." I knew that, but I appreciated that other people noticed it in me.

We wandered around for an hour and only found two of the three Sparks's siblings. Well, the ones present at the event, anyway. He has six siblings.

Riona and Niall—the twins—were entirely unhelpful. They had no interest in helping their older brother find "the ghost-loving cousin with frizzy red hair." Well, clearly, Sparks's descriptions did not aid in our search.

Because almost *every* Sparks has red hair. Apparently this cousin's dad is Mr. Sparks's brother.

The four of us stood in the foyer while the final donations were called. We escaped the ballroom for the big-ask but would return when they opened up the dance floor. I didn't think corporate galas did that. I thought it was just sitting around at a table eating caviar and talking numbers. You know. Boring stuff.

"Ughhhh," Sparks whined. "I'm still hungryyyy."

"Just go find your cousin and ask for food." Anderson said.

Bancroft toyed with his puzzle cube. Apparently he had it checked with his coat. "He can't find her."

"Yes, I can!" Sparks jumped up—a little too quickly. He grabbed his head and teetered back and forth.

"Dude, don't puke." I slid out of his firing range.

Sparks waved a hand at me. "Look, I know my dad or Brigid are around here somewhere."

"Do you know what your cousin's co-workers look like?" I asked. I didn't mind partying, but I wanted to talk to her about Ghost Girl before the alcohol enveloped every rational thought.

Sparks flailed his arms. "No, I don't. Okay? My cousins are redheads with freckles like me. Corporate Cousin's hair is so thick it looks like that Scottish princess. You can't miss her."

My heart fluttered. That was weird. Must have been the alcohol.

"Where is the DJ?" a female voice shouted.

That voice. My stomach flipped. She sounded just like her. The one I was looking for. Every frustrated tone sounded just like how she spoke to me the last day I saw her…

No. It wasn't her. It couldn't be.

"Kirk?" she shouted again.

Kirk? I know a Kirk. Well, I personally don't know him. But she knew him… And how could anyone forget a name like that?

"Yeah, yeah, keep your skirt, on Ms. Sparks," a man—Kirk, I supposed—snapped.

I jumped to my feet. "Did you hear what I heard?"

Anderson nodded. "Sounds like we found Corporate Cousin. She can lead us to ghost-story cousin. And maybe Sparks's dad."

I looked down the hall to my right where a brief argument ensued.

"Kirk, just go find him!" Ginger and blue flashed in the doorway.

The butterflies in my stomach fluttered. I placed my right hand on my chest. The scar left by Ghost Girl's touch throbbed. It *had* to be the alcohol.

"Thank you! Ugh, now where is my sister? She was supposed to be with Uncle Rowan." Ginger and blue flashed again.

Sparks's lips formed an *o*. He hopped up and down like a child who knew the answer to a math problem. "Oh, that's my dad's name!"

Anderson laughed. "I would've hoped you knew your dad's name."

Ms. Sparks marched down the hall. "She was supposed to wait!"

My heart leaped when I saw her. Sparks was right: she looked like the Scottish princess. Her blue gown swayed with every step like waves crashing against the shore. Curly ginger hair flew weightless behind her. Bright green eyes scanned the room, searching for the one she was waiting for.

"Wait, cousin!" Sparks yelled.

She didn't hear him and stormed past.

I caught a whiff of her perfume. I inhaled the scent. It was floral. It was earthy. It was… familiar.

My heart raced. The butterflies in my stomach went out of control.

She smelled like lavender and pine.

I stifled a gasp. My feet moved before my brain knew what was happening. Each step grew faster and faster. I had no control of my body. It moved on its own. Weightless as they chased after Ms. Sparks.

It couldn't be her.

She was dead.

She was a *ghost*.

Well, Ghost Girl *did* say she ran events. She *did* say she had a big one coming up. She *did* mention her annoying coworker Kirk never did anything right.

Could it be possible?

"Wait, Ms. Sparks!" I called out.

"I'm done waiting!" she shouted back.

Did she know it was me? No. She didn't. She rushed like a chicken with her head cut off. She had a job to do, and she would do it right.

"Please, I'm sorry!" I didn't know why those words flew out of my mouth, but there was no stopping them. They were an arrow soaring through the hall.

They found their mark. Ms. Sparks stopped. Her shoulders slumped and she turned around.

Her eyes widened. She saw me. She looked at me. Gently, she pressed a hand to her cheek, mirroring where my eye patch was. She glanced over her shoulder and back. A few hesitating steps and then ran up to me.

Her lips parted, but no words came out. She scanned me up and down as if she took in every detail of my appearance. "Wh-what? Wh-who?" Her fingers tangled in her hair. "A-are you?" Fingers extended, her hand reached for my face, but she hesitated.

My limbs tingled, but I lifted my arm. I pressed my hand against hers, wrapping my fingers around her palm. A jolt sent through my body. A light flashed before my eyes and faded. Warmth spread through my limbs. Comforting, joyful, familiar.

Was Ms. Sparks *the* Ghost Girl?

I squeezed her hand tighter. With all the bravery I could muster, I pressed her palm against my cheek. "I-I'm sorry, Ms. Sparks."

She inhaled sharply. After a brief moment, she rubbed her thumb along my cheekbone. She leaned forward, her breath tickled my chin.

One word escaped her lips. One word I never thought I'd hear from Corporate Cousin. One word that unraveled my being. "Second?"

Butterflies scattered in my stomach. The hair raised on my neck. This woman I never met knew my nickname. Outside of camp, I went by my first name. Second was a person only Southpaw knew.

I opened my mouth but ended up gawking like an idiot. I tried to make a better impression. I was dumbfounded. Stupified. Her beauty enamored me. Froze me. I thought of nothing else but her. The clamor of the crowd, the announcements of the presenter, none of it existed.

It was just me and Ghost Girl.

She smiled. A familiar grin that warmed my soul. Brought my heart out of despair back at Camp Southpaw.

"Nice to finally meet you, Second." Her soft fingers rubbed my cheek. "My name is Violetta Sparks."

The sound of her name and her gentle touch sent a wave of emotion through my body. Joy, gratitude, excitement, peace. I wanted to wrap my arms around her. Pull her in and tell her how sorry I was. How much I cared for her.

But I stood there like an idiot. The only sentence my brain could conceive tumbled from my lips:

"I'm Mason Piccirillo the Second. I've been waiting for you."

TO BE CONTINUED

He Loved Me through My Letters

A NOTE FROM THE AUTHOR

You weren't supposed to read this story.

This story started out as a fairytale retelling: my fairytale retelling. It was a short and sweet story for my husband, Paul (known as IV to most). To keep the real story short, he had worked three months out of the year at a Christian summer camp for boys. After he returned home in the summer of 2021, he met me. We began our relationship on September 10, 2021.

Then, in the summer of 2022 he went away for camp again, leaving me behind. No cell service, but we could communicate by letters.

So what did I do while he was away? I wrote him a book.

But after I completed it, I realized you needed to hear it, too.

A piece of my heart is wrapped up in this trilogy.

Not only is it Paul and my love story retold, it's our growing into ourselves.

It's our brokenness, sadness, and past pains splattered onto the pages of this book.

So, why share such a vulnerable story?

You need to know you're worth more than your scars.

You're worth more than the painful past that haunts your dreams.

You're worth more than the lies and deceit people throw upon you.

You are worthy, you are beautiful, you are loved.

And you don't need to earn any of it.

You are already enough.

With truth, hope, and strength,

Sara Francis

ACKNOWLEDGEMENTS

This story is in your hands because of the love and support I received from some beautiful people.

First, my critique crew, my gal pals, my favoritest author bunch: the Belletrists. Erin Forbes, R.C. Lloyd, and Jenni Sauer, I could not have done this without you three. You were present when my chaotic brain conceived this story. My late night Instagram messages, wild voice memos, and fangirling writing sessions meant so much more with you. Cheers to more sleepless nights and sticker creations.

Next, my sister-from-another-mister, Samantha. Sami, you think I'd leave you out of here? First off, my entire writing career stemmed from our random roleplay as kids. Now, here we are. Onto my second trilogy featuring more crazy kids like Huerta to add to The Terra Testimonies crew. Huerta may never get a standalone, but he will always be the main character in our hearts.

To my incredible editor, Angela Watts. The genuine joy, love, and hype you gave this story brought joy to my heart. Thank you for answering my midnight comments and questions—especially about italics because they confuse me. Your joy and love for this project inspired me to keep pushing, even when things grew difficult.

To the bookstagram community: thank you for your support, encouragement, hype, and guidance. You're the reason why I never tire of making reels.

My family, of course. Mom, Dad, Mary Grace, Therese, and Catherine, thanks for believing in me and inspiring the characters in this story. I can't wait for readers to meet Ghost Girl's family. You may see yourselves along the pages.

My husband, Paul. As I'm writing this acknowledgement, we're not married yet. But the fact that we're planning a wedding and you're helping me with a 12 month launch plan means more than you know. Thanks for letting me show you font sizes, asking you silly questions, reading aloud my story, being my main character, filming reels with me, and the list goes on. Thank you.

I owe all my talents to the One True King. Let my work sing His praises and my words reflect His own.

And finally, thank you for reading. I hope this story has touched your heart like it did mine. I said it in my note, and I'll say it again: you are worthy, you are beautiful, you are loved.

KICKSTARTER ACKNOWLEDGEMENTS

A special thanks to these amazing Kickstarter supporters.
Their support truly brought this book to life.

Addison Horner
Alane Middleton
Alexandra Corrsin
Ali Costa
Alisa J Maas
Amanda Auler
Amanda Balter
Amanda Hill
Angela R. Watts
Angelie Beauregard
Anna Cuccovia
Ariel Jackson
Asa Carmichael
Ashton Smith
Aunt Bonnie
Benita Thompson
Bianca Visic
Bramwell Crocker
Brandon H
Breanna Gipe
Brittany Wang
Brittney Nichols
Brooks Moses
Cameron Tidd
Casa Urraca Press
Catherine Gardner
Catherine Holmes

Cherelle Hopper
Christa Sheffield
Christina Tang-Bernas
Claire Banschbach
Claire Brucher
Connie Webster
Craig Francis
Dana A Caldwell
Danielle Huish
Darlene Böcek
David Holzborn
Deborah Raciti
Denise Mercer
Diego J Riley
Elizabeth Watanabe
Emma Hill
Eric Ostby
Erin Lane
Eron Wyngarde
Eugénie Legendre
Francesco Tehrani
Giselle Trejo
Greg Raciti
Hannah Jones
Helene Combes
Isabel Kishi
Jean Pace

Jen Woodrum
Jessica Micklethwaite
Jo Holloway
Joann Farrell
Josh Baron
Juan Manuel Nieto Campos
June Cali
Kassie Hayne
Katherine Setzer
Katherine Shipman
Katie B.C.
Kayla Ann
Kelly Moldenhauer
Kristen Altmann
Laura
Lauren Raciti
Leah C. Freeman
Luke Rispoli
Lydia Woodward
Mackenzie Clark
Maria Franchesca Caram
Maria L. Bement
Maria Zavala
Marin Ito
Meagan
Michaela Bush
Michelle
Michelle Gartner
Morgan Hagar
Moriah Baldwin
Natalie Colburn
Nena Yochim
Nicholas Stephenson

Nick Mandujano III
Nicola Thompson
Nicole Norrington
Nik Lamont
Olives Erickson
Pamela Hart
Robert
Robin
Robin Winckler
ROY Clémence
Ruth Dillon
S. W. Eon
S.F. Brooke
Samantha Mendell
Samantha Tucker
Sandra Merritt
Sara Koshofer
Sarah Porter
Sarah Schroeder
Serena Mire
Sergio Acuna
Sherry Mock
Simone Perry
Tabitha Gallemore
Tanya Bowers-Dean
Terri Raciti
BackerKit
Thomas Gallaway
Vickie L Grider
Victoria Clemm
Victoria Worley
Wendy Brown

ABOUT THE AUTHOR

Sara Francis has over 11 fiction publications. Her writing career started with The Terra Testimonies, a YA Dystopian trilogy for fans of The Hunger Games, X-Men, and Ender's Game. From there, her writing career evolved into writing children's books, poetry, short stories, and contemporary fiction. She hopes to make souls brighter and lives lighter through her stories. Her books are meant to inspire you to seek what is true, good, and beautiful, remembering you're loved and valued beyond measure.

When Francis isn't writing or working with clients through SF Publishing & Media, she spends time with her husband, works her day job at LEGOLAND® Resorts, or makes fun reels for her bookstagram page. She is a coffee addict (too many cups a day) and will stay up late playing games or chatting with the Belletrists. French Fries are her favorite food and she believes everyone deserves little treats.

Her favorite story tropes are found family, slow burn romance, "Who did this to you?", secret identity, stupid humor, and love triangles (I know, controversial).

At the end of the day, she wants to inspire others to become the best version of themselves, enjoying this life to the fullest until it's time for the next.

KEEP IN TOUCH WITH SARA FRANCIS ON
SOCIAL MEDIA

SaraFrancis_Author

SaraFrancisAuthor

SaraFrancisAuthor

PLEASE SUBSCRIBE TO HER NEWSLETTER
TO STAY UP TO DATE

WWW.SARA-FRANCIS.COM/SUBSCRIBE

CONSIDER LEAVING A REVIEW ON GOODREADS
AND AMAZON TO SPREAD THE WORD ABOUT
SHE WHISPERED THROUGH THE WOODS

SCAN FOR QUICK LINKS!

SOUTHPAW STICKY BUNS

Chef Jeff's Secret Recipes

INGREDIENTS

Dough
- 1¼ cups hot milk about 110F/ 43 C
- ¼ cup warm water
- 1 packet instant dry yeast
- ¼ cup sugar
- 1 large egg at room temperature
- ¼ cup butter melted
- 3 to 4 cups all-purpose/plain flour
- 1 teaspoon salt

Filling
- 4 tablespoons melted butter
- ¼ cup light brown sugar
- ¼ cup granulated sugar
- 2 tablespoons ground cinnamon

Topping
- ½ cup butter (about 1 stick)
- 1 cup light brown sugar
- ½ cup honey (or maple syrup)
- 2 tablespoons whipping cream

inspired by Erren's Kitchen

INSTRUCTIONS

1. Dissolve yeast in a small bowl of warm water and set aside.
2. Mix milk, sugar, melted butter, salt, and egg
3. Add 2 cups of flower and mix until smooth. Add yeast. Mix in the rest of the flour until dough is easy to work with
4. Knead dough on lightly floured surface for 5-10 minutes. Place in an oiled bowl, cover, and leave to rise until doubled in size (about 2-3 hours)
5. In a saucepan over medium heat, add the butter, brown sugar, and honey, stirring until melted and bubbling. This will be the topping.
6. Remove from heat, add cream, mix well. Pour into a greased 9x13 inch pan and set aside.
7. In a small bowl, mix butter, sugar, brown sugar, and cinnamon. This will be the filling.
8. Punch down the dough then roll out onto a floured surface into a 15 by 9 inch rectangle. Spread the filling over the rolled dough. Beginning on the long side, roll up the dough and pinch edges to seal. Cut into 10-12 slices.
9. Place sliced buns into the pan with the topping (about 2 inches apart) and let rise util they've doubled in size (about 30 minutes to an hour).
10. Pre-heat oven to 350f/175c.
11. Bake for 20-30 minutes or until golden brown. Let cool before flipping to serve sticky side up.

SECOND'S SONG SELECTS

southpaw hype

- Love Runs Out - One Republic
- Shotgun - George Ezra
- Tonight Tonight - Hot Chelle Rae
- All the Small Things - blink-182
- High School Never Ends - Bowling for Soup
- Burn the House Down - AJR
- Live Like We're Dying - Kris Allen
- Year 3000 - Jonas Brothers

get our legs movin' on a hike

- Pump Up The Jam - Technotronic
- World's Smallest Violin - AJR
- Uptown Funk - Mark Ronson, Bruno Mars
- Are You Gonna Be My Girl - Jet
- Everybody Talks - Neon Trees
- Walk This Way - Aerosmith
- Thunderstruck - AC/DC
- Livin' On A Prayer - Bon Jovi

every Cub after the first 10 miles

huerta's meme-song-repertoire

- Ring of Fire - Johnny Cash
- Never Gonna Give You Up - Rick Astley
- Photograph - Nickelback
- Peaches - Jack Black
- Bring Me To Life - Evanescence
- All Star - Smash Mouth
- Windows XP Startup Sound - Microsoft
- Shooting Stars - Bag Raiders
- Loverboy - A-Wall
- The X-Files Theme - Mark Snow
- Deja Vu - Initial D
- In the Hall of the Mountain King - Edvard Grieg

songs for the campfire

- By and By - Caamp
- Knee Deep - Zac Brown Band
- Chicken Fried - Zac Brown Band
- Rockstar Sea Shanty - Nickelback
- Drive All Night - NEEDTOBREATHE
- Ho Hey - Lumineers
- Hold back the River - James Bay
- Campfire Song - Spongebob Squarepants

when my thoughts hurt too much

- You'd Be Paranoid Too - Waterparks
- Dead to Me - Futuristic, Loveless
- The Stigma (Boys Don't Cry) - AS IT IS
- Better Than This - Set It Off
- Ghosts - Lukr
- Certified Depressant - Taylor Acorn
- I Wanna Get Better - ATC, The Ready Set

when I daydream of her

- My Heart I Surrender - I Prevail
- Set of 2 - Brandon Lake
- Oxygen - Hometown Losers
- Hand to Hold - Ryan Proudfoot
- Steal My Girl - One Direction
- Like No One Does - Jake Scott
- Take It All Back 2.0 - Judah & the Lion
- Falling Further Faster - Sleep On It
- break my heart - Matt Hansen
- Like No One Does - Jake Scott
- Ghost - Like Ghosts
- She Looks So Perfect - 5 Seconds of Summer
- If You Love Her - Forest Blakk, Meaghan Trainor
- Safe - Antoine Bradford

CAMP SOUTHPAW

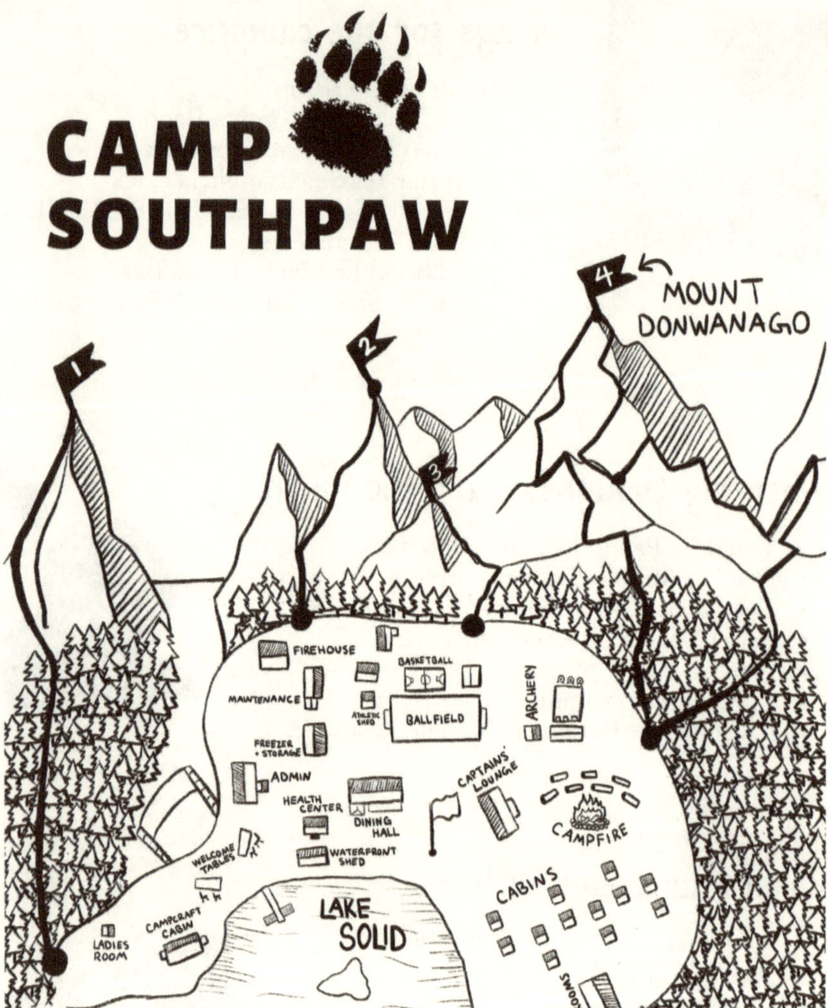

Founded in 1930, Southpaw leads boys into the wilderness to explore what it means to be men. We captains build personal relationships with our cubs, encouraging them to grow physically, mentally, socially, and spiritually. We connect personally with each other, we encourage one another along the trail, and we make memories that are passed down from generation to generation.